THE HENCHMEN OF ZENDA

KJ CHARLES

Published by KJC Books

The Henchmen of Zenda

Cover art: Simoné, dreamarian.com
Layout: L.C. Chase, lcchase.com/design.htm

ISBN: 978-1-912688-00-5

First edition
June, 2018

Also available in ebook:
ISBN: 978-1-9997846-9-0

THE HENCHMEN OF ZENDA

KJ CHARLES

TABLE OF CONTENTS

Publisher's Note 1

Cast of Characters 3

Chapter 1 5

Chapter 2 15

Chapter 3 23

Chapter 4 31

Chapter 5 41

Chapter 6 53

Chapter 7 65

Chapter 8 75

Chapter 9 85

Chapter 10 95

Chapter 11 105

Chapter 12 115

Chapter 13 123

Chapter 14 133

Chapter 15 143

Chapter 16 155

Chapter 17 165

Chapter 18 175

Author's Note 185

PUBLISHER'S NOTE

The papers here presented, which have been lodged in a bank vault for many years under the simple but unhelpful instruction, "Wait until everyone is dead," purport to be the memoirs of Mr. Jasper Detchard and are, in the author's words, "a response" to the account of the Ruritanian succession crisis written by Mr. Rudolf Rassendyll, and later published as *The Prisoner of Zenda*.

The Publisher is aware that the present history casts the gravest doubt on both the veracity of Mr. Rassendyll and the honour of the present Ruritanian royal family, and makes no assertion whatsoever as to the truth of Mr. Detchard's tale. We present it solely as a fictional artefact, and any complaints about the contents, requests for withdrawal, or legal threats should be made directly to our solicitors.

CAST OF CHARACTERS

The Royal Family
　Rudolf Elphberg, Crown Prince of Ruritania
　Michael Elphberg, Duke of Strelsau, half brother to Rudolf
　Flavia Elphberg, Princess of the Blood, cousin to Michael and
　Rudolf

Team Rudolf
　Colonel Sapt, a military man
　Fritz von Tarlenheim, gentleman-in-waiting
　Rudolf Rassendyll, a passing Englishman

Team Michael
　Jasper Detchard, a henchman
　Rupert von Hentzau, a cad
　Bersonin, a poisoner
　Lauengram, a minor noble
　De Gautet, a swordsman
　Krafstein, a pimp
　Antoinette de Mauban, Michael's mistress

CHAPTER ONE

W hen I read a story, I skip the explanations; yet the moment I begin to write one, I find that I must have an explanation.

This is Rudolf Rassendyll's introduction to his swashbuckling tale of intrigue, love, treachery, cold-blooded murder, and hot-blooded men. His account, privately circulated, has become the accepted truth amongst the few privileged to read it. It is a story of courage in the dark, honour in the teeth of love, nobility above all. It gives us a beautiful, passionate princess, a man who renounces love and crown for the sake of a greater and purer cause, and a villain—*such* a villain. Rupert of Hentzau: reckless and wary, graceful and graceless, handsome, debonair, vile, and unconquered. Rupert flees the pages of Rassendyll's story a thwarted monster, never to be seen again; Rassendyll retires from the field with honour unstained; and the true King of Ruritania reigns in Strelsau.

What a pile of shit.

My name is Jasper Detchard, and according to Rassendyll's narrative I am dead. This should give you some idea of his accuracy, since I do not dictate these words to some cabbage-scented medium from beyond the veil. There is no doubt that I *will* be dead by the time anyone reads these pages—in fact, it is absolutely necessary that should be the case, as my words would earn me the inconvenience of a very long prison sentence or a very short drop, and moreover the fate of a kingdom could be swayed by my words. But I am, as I write, alive, well, and irritated. There is a long railway journey ahead of me, a glass of brandy to my hand, and a heavily and obscenely annotated copy of the Rassendyll manuscript by my side. I intend to use them all to tell the truth.

My name is Jasper Detchard. I was born to a well-off family in the outskirts of—oh dear God, must I? It is customary in these accounts to rehearse one's family history in vast detail over three generations, but I am quite sure my reader is, if possible, even less interested in my paternal grandmother than I am. To hell with it.

My name is not Jasper Detchard. Obviously it is not. I had another name once, but I stained it at school with various crimes, culminating in a sufficiently serious indiscretion that my parents declined to give me the opportunity of being thrown out of a university too, and disposed of me via the Army and a posting to India. This suited me well, since England is too small for my fancy and too moralistic for my tastes. Unfortunately, the Army brought Englishness with it, and to cut a long and doubtless shocking story short, I was cashiered. I left the Army with numerous prizes for swordplay, a dishonourable discharge, a reputation for cheating at cards (fairly earned), another for indulgence in the fuck that dare not speak its name (ditto), and a request from my family that I no longer claim kinship with them, since they wanted none with me. I did them that service and named myself Detchard, after the first town where I sucked a man off, and Jasper, because if one's lot in life is to be a Victorian villain, one might as well play the game properly.

So there I was, rootless, wandering, rebaptised into a new life without family or history. I worked my way back from India using my cards, wits, and blade, but did not trouble England's shores. The Continent is a more welcoming place for my sort of people: adventurers, wanderers, gentleman thieves and gentleman thugs, ladies of the day and night, gamblers and fences and information brokers, aristocrats brought low, masquerading commoners reaching dangerously high. We of that tribe drift in and out of lives and languages and countries, a loose fraternity of rogues with a looser tangle of loyalties and rivalries, and one may see the same face over the course of years in a Berlin nightspot, a Prague palace, and a Roman gaol.

To give a single example: I was in Vienna when I first met a very pretty Frenchwoman of seventeen flaunted as mistress by a dishonest stockbroker three times her age. I next encountered her when I was hired as bravo at an extremely elegant and accommodating brothel in Dresden where she presided over the festivities. She recognised me at once—unsurprisingly, as I had killed her first protector in front of her—but she was utterly charming about the whole business, assuring me that she had found him as tiresome as the people who had hired me to do it. We worked together for a highly entertaining eighteen months, until she accepted an ambassador's carte blanche, and I decided to sell my blade to a more generous bidder. Three years later, when I lay in a Paris gaol cell awaiting the inevitable discovery of a single, deadly proof of my guilt and the equally inevitable trip to Madame Guillotine, it was my pretty Frenchwoman to whom I wrote in desperation, and she who bailed and bribed me out, at eye-watering cost. Such is the demimonde life, where risks and passions run high, true friendships are as precious and as rare as diamonds, and morals are an inconvenience.

That is Mr. Jasper Detchard for you, take him or leave him, and that was the man sought out by Michael Elphberg that chilly autumn. Michael, Duke of Strelsau, second son to Rudolf IV of Ruritania. Michael, who would be king.

I really am going to have to do the explanations now.

Ruritania is a small kingdom nestled in the heart of Europe, to the south-east of Germany, a mountainous, forested, picturesque little place of some strategic importance thanks to its location and defensible mountainous borders. For the last two centuries it has been ruled by the Elphberg dynasty, a family noted for their blue eyes and striking dark red hair. You may wander through the picture galleries of the palace at Strelsau and see blue-eyed, red-haired Elphbergs going back to their humble beginnings as mere dukes. Red is the hue of royalty in Ruritania: as the old saying has it, "If he's red, he's right!"

I invite you to consider what this means. For a family to remain red-headed and blue-eyed down three centuries, in a land not filled with redheads or aristocrats, requires either careful breeding or a failure to grasp simple principles of stock management. Given the nearby example of the Hapsburg royal family, whose twisted family tree ended in a wretched lunatic whose grandmother was also his aunt, one might think the Elphbergs would have considered their habit of cousin-marriage more carefully, but as these pages will show, you can't tell a Ruritanian aristocrat anything.

Some thirty years before our story starts, Ruritania's King Rudolf IV married his first cousin, who made up in red hair and blue eyes what she lacked in stamina, brains, or chin. She gave him a sickly brat of a son, also Rudolf (every second person in this damned tale is called Rudolf, for which I can only apologise), and promptly expired, her duty done. The King, evidently not racked by grief, married again with what sticklers regarded as indecent haste, this time to a woman of no significant birth from near the southern border. She had dark hair and a hell of a temper, and I expect she had a great deal to be angry about, in part because her marriage was morganatic. (That is to say, the difference in rank between husband and wife was such that any offspring would not be automatically heir to the father's titles.) If one had to be married to an Elphberg, one really would want to get the benefits.

This would not have been a great problem if the new wife had had daughters. Fate being what it is, she produced a son, a child who inherited her looks and was just two years younger than the royal heir. The boys quickly became known as Red Rudolf and Black Michael, very much in keeping with the Brothers Grimm landscape that is Ruritania. I will tell you this: none of us there was snow white.

The boys learned to hate one another before they learned to speak. Michael was sturdy and daring and beloved by their father where Rudolf was pallid and fearful, so Rudolf hated Michael. But Rudolf was a prince where Michael was nothing, so Michael hated Rudolf, with a passion that smouldered in him the more strongly as Rudolf's failings became more apparent. He was a puling, indulged, nasty, malicious brat, but he was the older, and the pure-blood red Elphberg, and so he would be king.

The brothers grew to manhood on no better terms. Michael had the title of Duke of Strelsau bestowed upon him at his fifteenth year—Strelsau, the capital itself. The old king could scarcely have made his preference clearer, yet Rudolf was still heir to the crown. The bad blood between the brothers did not lessen over this partiality.

They fought. They fought over servants, and allies, and women, always women. If one wanted a woman, the other must needs have her—ideally by seduction (since to steal a heart was a greater triumph than to issue a command or to take by force), but they were the prince and the duke, and Rudolf in particular could do precisely as he chose.

Except in the case of Her Royal Highness Princess Flavia, the future queen.

Flavia was cousin (of course) to the brothers, next heir of the Blood after Prince Rudolf. Her father, having somewhat more sense than the majority of his family, had scoured Europe for the best-born unrelated redhead he could discover, and produced a healthy girl of appropriate colouring and admirable vigour. She had as much beauty as a wealthy princess requires, and significantly more brain, and her destiny, never doubted, was to wed the future king, whoever he might be.

I don't know if Red Rudolf wanted her for herself. I doubt it; I am not aware he ever saw a woman as more than a place to put his prick, or a way to confound his brother. I know that Michael wanted her hand to make himself royal, and her heart to prove that he could win something Rudolf never would. For Flavia aged eleven had come upon Rudolf aged fifteen, carefully practising his knifework on a cat that he had pinned to the ground for greater convenience, and Flavia did not wish to marry her prince at all.

Imagine Ruritania at the time of which I write. Rudolf, in his early thirties now, is dissipated, self-indulgent, drinking and wenching, with an erratic temper that even loyal courtiers struggle to laugh away as simply due to his red hair. He has spent a great deal of his last years outside the country on his father's command, indulging his appetites and oddities where his people cannot see him, but even so his reputation is known, and the lower orders hide their daughters away when the prince rides. Michael, by contrast, rules as duke in Strelsau with care and wisdom. He has a temper, but he controls it. He no longer competes with his brother over conquests; he is punctilious in his respect to the future king; he plays the man while his brother plays the fool. The old king is sick, a slow decline that will not stop. And the whispers spread across Ruritania: Might he choose Michael? Could he debar Rudolf from the succession? Suppose he wed Michael to Flavia now? What if? Could he? Will they?

If he's red, he's right! insists the countryside, especially the parts where Rudolf doesn't ride, but there is shifting and murmuring in the narrow, turbulent streets of the Old Town of Strelsau, where Michael is felt to be one of them, and the people dream of change.

That, then, is your explanation, and I could have saved a deal of words if I had written simply, *Two brothers, one crown.*

It was a week or so after my thirty-sixth birthday, a chilly autumn night. I was staying in the sole inn of a small and unimportant village some way south of Dresden, recovering from a trifling wound I had incurred in my rapid departure from the city (the word *flight* is so undignified), and I had a fire blazing, my feet up, a glass of good red wine in one hand and an unexpurgated volume of Catullus in the other. I heard noise on the old wooden stairs, but it was not of the kind to cause a watchful man alarm: neither the firm tread of police nor, worse, the surreptitious sounds of stealth. He came openly up the stairs, chatting with his companions like any guest, and I will admit I was quite startled when the door opened and a man came in.

"I beg your pardon, sir," I said. "The room is reserved."

He did not leave; rather, he shut the door behind him. I put my feet down, intending to stand in case I had to fight. He waved a hand at me to retain my seat, for all the world as though he were bidding me to spare a courtesy. "Please, don't get up, Mr. Detchard," he said. "Or should I address you as Mr. —?" And he used the name that I had stained and abandoned like a rag.

I started up from my chair at that. He shook his head with sublime confidence. "I have two men outside, Mr. Detchard—if you prefer that name—and no intention of doing you injury. Perhaps I should introduce myself. I am Michael, Duke of Strelsau." He smiled at whatever he saw in my face. "Do sit."

How to describe Michael? He was thirty or so years of age with dark curly hair, not much above the medium height but well built, bearing himself with command. His dress lacked all ostentation: it was that of a gentleman who could afford plainness. He was not armed. He had no guards. He was a predator.

I think I have conveyed something of what I am. I had other men's money in my pocket and other men's blood on my hands; I made a living outside the law and did not let that fact disturb my sleep. I know danger as an intimate friend, and when I looked at Michael, I saw it. Not physical danger—I was the taller and stronger, and would learn that he was no more than adequate with a blade or pistol. But I am a killer by trade, and I know the look of a man who commands death—more than that, of one who enjoys doing it.

I obeyed orders, and sat. His Grace of Strelsau took a chair opposite. We regarded one another.

I have told you what I saw. What he saw . . . Well, let me once again quote Rassendyll, who speaks of *the Englishman, Detchard, a narrow-faced fellow, with close-cut fair hair and a bronzed complexion. He was a finely made man, broad in the shoulder and slender in the hips. A good fighter, but a crooked customer.* That is how Rassendyll saw me, and I will only say, it takes one to know one, you red-haired prick.

Michael steepled his fingers and began to speak. His subject was the Life and Works of Jasper Detchard, and he covered it in detail. One may do almost anything with a man by making him the centre of attention, but generally the aim is to flatter, and Michael did not flatter me. He spoke of my expulsion from Rugby, my chequered career in the Army (including certain events that would have got me worse than cashiering had they been public knowledge), and some of my more recent history, in vast and incriminating detail, even down to that unfortunate recent contretemps in Dresden. He told me in so many words that he had the knowledge to hang me, the will to use it, and the forces at his command to overpower me no matter how I might resist. Even now I can feel the smart of that one-sided conversation as he made his mastery over me humiliatingly clear.

With another man, I might have put his claims to the test: dealt with the swine and gone for the window over his body. I did not think of doing so now. I merely sat, mute and trapped, as he concluded his recital. "All told, yours has been an adventurous career."

"And are you here to put it to an end?" I replied somewhat sullenly.

Michael smiled. "That would be a waste. You seem to me a man of firmness. You are decisive. You act. Unlawfully, criminally, even, but a man of action is better than a waverer or a wastrel. There are two things I wish to know of you, Mr. Detchard. Can you take orders? And can you give loyalty?"

"I have never tried to do either."

"No, I don't suppose you have." His eyes held mine, dark gaze boring into me. I had no doubt he could order my death with a snap of his fingers and feel no more remorse than for swatting a fly, and something deep and dark within me responded intensely to that awareness.

"What do you want?" I asked him.

"I want your service. Your obedience without question, your loyalty without reserve, your right arm as though it were my own. You will be my man, Mr. Detchard, and as my man you will be everyone else's master. There will be no impertinent questions from the Munich police, no spying servants to threaten you with tiresome laws. If you are the duke's man in public, you may do as you please in private. I suspect you will find that as attractive as the salary."

"Which is?"

He mentioned a sum.

I whistled. "You pay generously."

"I pay for absolute loyalty. I would say also for the risks you will undoubtedly run in my service, but I imagine danger will be a draw rather than a disadvantage to you."

"You seem to know me well, considering this is our first meeting."

"I have had my eye on you for some time. I have a list of seven. Your name is third upon it."

"Really," I said, somewhat stung. "May I know whose are first and second?"

Michael smiled. He felt confident then that he had me, I suppose. "First is Bersonin."

"The Belgian?" I had not met him, but he was known in my circles for his tricks with strange powders and medicines that did little good to their takers.

"Indeed. Second, Albert von Lauengram—you will not know of him, a countryman of mine, well connected. Then yourself, of course, and the Frenchman de Gautet."

I lifted a brow. "I see I am keeping good company."

"I had a Boer hunter in mind, a marvellous shot, but he proved too provincial in his outlook." Michael gave a dismissive wave. "There is also Krafstein, another Ruritanian, and I have approached a countryman of yours, a man of interesting talents. He is a cricketer. I know you English enjoy that."

Freedom from cricket was one of the many reasons I was glad to be an exile. I prayed it would not be inflicted on me, as I would be forced to respond with violence. "So your attendance will consist of six gentlemen-in-waiting?" I asked.

"That is my intention. I have a final candidate if the Englishman does not serve. Is your shoulder sufficiently recovered to ride?"

"I dare say."

"Good. Papers will be delivered to you by the morning. You will come to me in Strelsau in two days' time. You will not fail me. Failure in my service is harshly punished, just as success is rewarded. And do not forget this one thing . . ." He leaned forwards and beckoned me to do the same. I obeyed, and found my chin taken in a grasp so firm that the fingers dug into my flesh. "I can have you hanged at a snap of my fingers, whenever I choose, or I can reward you far beyond your imaginings. Your life is mine to do with as I please, and you will use it for me." He released me as abruptly and smiled at me, or at my lack of violent response, with curling satisfaction. "You are welcome to my household, Detchard."

No courtesy for me in the duke's service, I saw. I inclined my head. "I am Your Grace's humble servant."

"Yes," Michael said. "You are."

CHAPTER TWO

Michael was as good as his word. He usually was when it was to his benefit. Within a week, I was comfortably installed in his household at Zenda and finding out the true nature of the man I was obliged to call master.

I must pause for explanation once more, since the geography of the country is relevant to my tale. Ruritania is not a large land, and boasts only one city: Strelsau, the capital and Michael's ducal seat. Strelsau is a divided city, not unlike Edinburgh, with a New Town and an Old. The shining, stately New Town, dominated by the palace, was the king's domain, where the upper classes strolled. The Old Town was picturesque but poor, a place of dark alleys and low, winding byways, and it belonged in heart to Michael, the placeless and resentful.

Although Michael was Duke of Strelsau, he had only a large and luxurious townhouse there. His great palace, held in his father's gift, was at Zenda, a small town fifty miles from the capital and about ten from the German frontier. Zenda is in the foothills of the greater mountains, the castle set on high ground overlooking the town at a little distance, and surrounded by large tracts of forest.

The castle of Zenda will play a large part in my tale, and it is necessary to understand the layout, so I hope the reader has a greater patience for description than I usually do.

The castle had begun life as a fortress in the sixteenth century, and still retained an imposing stone tower, surrounded by a deep and wide moat. In front of that now stood a handsome modern chateau, and this was Michael's country residence. A broad and welcoming avenue led up to the front of the modern chateau; the only means of entry to the old Tower at its back was to cross the moat by means of a drawbridge. This had been rebuilt in recent years so that it was raised and lowered from the chateau's side of the moat, not from the Tower. Thus, when the drawbridge was up, the old building became an unassailable and inescapable prison, since even if the people inside it jumped into the water, it was not possible for a man to climb out of the steep-sided moat unaided. The Elphbergs had turned a secure defensive retreat for themselves into a prison for others; this says a certain amount about both their confidence and their attitude to rule.

Schloss Zenda is a magnificent blend of ancient and modern, and if the reader, unlike your humble narrator, is able to cross the Ruritanian border without risking execution, I should highly recommend a sightseeing trip. The chateau when I lived there was a fine house in the French style, with modern conveniences and costly furnishings. Gilt and mirrors, windows and broad hallways, painting and sculpture, grace and dignity. It reflected Michael's public face, which smiled upon the world like a noble gentleman. Here Michael received guests, entertained visitors, and managed his household and his estates in a way that advertised how he would manage a kingdom. The staff were respectful but content, the maids pretty but untouched, the house magnificent but welcoming. One could not visit the chateau of Zenda without admiring its master.

No casual guests visited the old moated building, and if the name of the Tower makes you think of the grim ancient prison that stands in London, it should. The Tower was medieval, not modern; dark and dank, not light and airy. It was a place of shadows and secrets, of ancient doors with heavy bars, of stone walls left bare because it was not a place of display, but one of truth—truth pulled out at the end of pliers or hot pokers, if need be. To dwell in the Tower was to understand Michael Elphberg, our duke of dark corners, and to fear him.

The few servants admitted to the Tower were hand-picked for their loyalty and their silence. The run of the place was given only to Michael's henchmen—his Five, as we were at the time of my arrival. We had rooms in the chateau but generally spent our leisure time in the Tower, where Michael liked to keep us. It was not unlike being a hound in a kennel.

I should introduce my four colleagues. First and most obtrusive was Bersonin the poisoner, bald as an egg, with soft fingers and an ingratiating manner of speech. I do not have high standards, but Bersonin disgusted me at a deep and visceral level. He took a kind of cold, clinical pleasure in killing; he liked to watch pain and to inflict it; he thought about little else than what he could do to unwilling bodies. De Gautet, a Frenchman whom I already knew slightly, was a far better companion. He was an excellent swordsman, sported a waxed moustache that was in my opinion a greater crime than any he committed with the blade, and had no sense of humour, but he was tolerable. Lauengram, of a minor Ruritanian noble family, was a decent fighter and gave us a thin veneer of respectability thanks to his good birth; his countryman Krafstein was our quartermaster and pimp. His role was to keep the Tower comfortable and as such he procured girls (from over the frontier, well paid, and warned to accommodate Bersonin's unpleasant tastes). He told me as much when I had been in the Tower just a few days, hailing my attention as I stood by the fire in the stone-walled room in which we dined or played cards.

"Cold, Detchard?"

Of course I was bloody cold; we were in a stone room in the shadow of the mountain in winter. "Not at all."

Krafstein smiled. "Perhaps I could assist you in keeping warm?"

"I regret you're not my type," I told him, mostly out of ill temper, though it had the merit of being true.

The smile didn't falter. "Nor you mine, I assure you. If you would care to advise me of your preferences, I will ensure you have companionship to your liking."

"You might find my tastes difficult to satisfy."

"I doubt that. Michael's man is everyone's master. Or, if you prefer *not* to be master in the bedroom, that can be arranged too." I raised a brow. He smiled more widely. "Let us be frank. Boys, girls, both. Any age or type, experience or none. One who will give you all the attention you desire, or ones who are . . . disposable. His Grace is keen that your leisure time should be satisfactory, and that there should be no unpleasantness outside the walls of the Tower. That, we leave to Red Rudolf."

I had already heard of the prince's unsavoury habits, and been warned that Michael tolerated no such thing in his own household. No Zenda innkeeper complained of a violated daughter, still less son, at the hands of Michael's men; the punctilious chivalry he demanded of us all down to the stable boys was part of his quiet campaign for Ruritania's love. I wondered how long it would last if he were crowned.

"No unpleasantness outside the Tower," I said. "And what about inside?"

"Here, dear fellow, you may be as beastly as you choose, so long as it is with partners of my provision. Discretion is all. What may I do for you?"

"I'm not that desperate yet," I told him. "Thank you for your offer. There is no need to repeat it."

He cocked his head. "Permit me to be clear. The law in Ruritania does not forbid your pleasures, so long as the boy is over thirteen and can be persuaded not to cry rape—"

"I don't fuck children."

"—but good society expects discretion. Michael's man may not prowl Zenda for boys, or even grown men. That is not a habit with which His Grace of Strelsau should be associated. And—kindly let me finish—Michael does not tolerate divided loyalty. Learn that, Detchard, and don't imagine yourself striking up some romance with a townsman; it will not end well. If Michael asks you to cut your brother's throat or your lover's, you will do it. His Grace is a jealous god, and you are his."

"What an extraordinary speech," I said. "Allow me to make one in return. I manage my own affairs; I shall never be sufficiently desperate to seek satisfaction from your hands; I am not here for romance. I dare say you are a very excellent procurer, as these things go, but I have no need for your services or your advice, and if you offer them again you will feel the toe of my boot. I trust I make myself clear."

Krafstein had gone rather pale. "Admirably."

"Then I bid you good day."

I have always had a knack for making friends.

Possibly the foregoing may lead you to believe I have at least the virtue of abstemiousness. I do not. It is simply that I am not in the habit of doing what is good for me, and I had no interest whatsoever in the tepid satisfaction of Krafstein's hand-picked whores. I prefer my excitements to *be* exciting, and if I inclined to women I should probably have pursued duchesses, or nuns, or the wives and daughters of the nation's most skilled duellists. The prospect of sticking my prick in some whimpering guttersnipe whose only ambition is to be paid . . . faugh. That is no improvement on my own two hands.

(I am requested to observe here that I don't actually need both hands at once. That was not my implication, and you will kindly stop looking over my blasted shoulder.)

As the reader will gather, I had not taken a liking to Krafstein, let alone Bersonin. De Gautet entirely lacked a sense of humour, but he could give me a decent match on the practice field, and Lauengram was a reasonable fellow with whom one could drink. We never got the other Englishman, so I was spared the boredom of cricket.

I had not expected my companions to be particularly congenial: men of our stamp rarely are. We were not permitted to fight one another except on the practice ground, so casual insults became a matter of routine instead of vengeance and quickly ceased to matter. We rubbed along with one another because Michael would have it so. We rode out with him, a proud retinue in the winding streets of the Old Town of Strelsau, a bodyguard in the New Town, since there was no more trust between the royal brothers than there was love. We talked to certain people on his behalf—those who might have spoken slightingly of his parentage, say, or those who were loud in their belief that the country should become a republic. We slouched in the shadows when he had delicate conversations with certain semi-official men whose German was of Berlin rather than Strelsau, and we discouraged the hangers-on and listeners with whom Rudolf plagued his brother, just as Michael did him.

That was the most important article of Michael's service: that we should loathe Prince Rudolf as much as Michael did. I found no difficulty in that, and raised my glass to his early demise with as much enthusiasm as any, because Rudolf was loathsome. One should never expect much of princes, but Rudolf was dissipated, self-indulgent, and what was worst, stupid. He treated his people with negligence bordering on contempt, and sometimes with those bright, sharp flashes of cruelty about which courtiers muttered behind closed doors. The old king knew of it, I dare say, but since his own right to rule came from his Elphberg blood, he could or would not declare his son's to be unfit. The nobles did not wish to know, because the only alternative was the commoner Michael, and they did not have to know because Rudolf had not yet been sufficiently uncontrolled to hurt a girl of importance, or take a whip to a senator's face instead of a shopkeeper's. They told each other that marriage and kingship would settle him down, as though he were eighteen rather than thirty-two, and as if the combination of privilege, indulgence, freedom from retaliation, and drink would not have corrupted a far wiser man. I rode in attendance a few times when Michael met his brother, and saw quite enough of Rudolf to make me conclude that the world would be a better place without him.

Michael didn't order a murder. I had assumed that would be my purpose, but he was not so straightforward.

"We can't kill the fool," he said one night—I think Bersonin had suggested some poison that would mimic the symptoms of liver failure. It was the depths of winter, and we dined in the Tower, for private speech. The wind whipped the ancient stone walls and rattled in the deep, narrow window slits. A fire roared in the great blackened hearth, and the five of us sat around the oak dining table with our master at its head. "If he dies, a portion of the country will blame me, however it is achieved. A fall from a horse, a sickness, or a duel—it will be put to my account, and the Red faction will rise against me."

Lauengram coughed delicately. "Not if you wed the Princess Flavia. She is dearly loved by the people, and the Senate."

"But I am not dearly loved by her," Michael said. "My father could command her to marry me, but he is a sentimental fool and he has listened to her pleas. He would name me heir if Rudolf died, but he is too frightened to force the issue or even strengthen my hand by making Flavia marry me. The damned decrepit weak old man."

"Yet if Red Rudolf does not die," Bersonin said, "he lives."

I refrained from throwing a piece of apple at him only because of the seriousness of the topic. De Gautet drawled, "Yes, that is evident."

"It is the heart of the matter. If Rudolf does not die he will be king, and if he becomes king, he will wife and father, and his child will be heir. So die he must. No?" (Bersonin was a Belgian, so I see no reason he should not have spoken better German than he did. Lauengram insisted that he simply liked to appear odd, and I can only say that if that was true, he must have been a singularly happy man.)

"Rudolf must certainly die before he marries, for our purposes," de Gautet said, meaning Michael's hopes of kingship. "If he spawns a son, the game is—fini."

"To win he must marry," Lauengram agreed. "But for him to be truly safe, his bride must be the Princess Flavia, and that is his problem. Until she becomes his wife, Flavia will be a threat to him. As an unmarried princess, she would be able to sway the Senate against him, should his madness progress to the point where he requires confinement. She could call for that, and even act as Regent, without incurring the, uh, the inevitable suspicions that would be cast upon our duke for making the same observation. So he must marry her or be at risk."

"Could she not have him confined once they were married?" I asked.

"In Ruritanian law, a wife cannot bear witness against her husband. It would be—not impossible, no, but very hard for her to enforce his confinement, and once he is king, who else would dare? No, if he can persuade her to take his hand, he will be safe."

"Unlike her," I remarked. "I should not care to be at Red Rudolf's mercy were I a woman."

Krafstein muttered something uncomplimentary. Michael hissed annoyance. "Cease this chatter, and be damned to talk of marriage. Listen. We do not kill Rudolf. Indeed, we shall watch his life with the tenderest care. We extend courtesies to him—not pretended love, which would fool nobody, but all that civility and custom demand. We build our duchy in such a way that no man can accuse us of higher ambition. You—all of you—will treat my brother's adherents and name with the respect due to a future king, not out of love, but upon my command. Do you hear me?" He looked around, meeting our eyes one by one. "From this moment, you, though you remain my men body and soul, understand that Rudolf will be king. I accept my brother's rule as his loyal servant. I kneel to kiss his hand."

He spoke those words of submission in a tone so chilling that I felt as though the room had darkened, as though he could put the lights out with the smothering force of his hatred. Nobody spoke for a long moment. Finally I asked, "And then what, Your Grace?"

"And then, Detchard, we wait. We wait for the wedding, if it comes first, or my father's death and the announcement of my brother's coronation. We do not act until that day. But when it comes . . ."

He had been preparing an apple as we spoke. Another man would have thrown the fruit at the wall, perhaps, or stabbed it with the silver paring knife. Michael slipped the viciously sharp little blade under the skin, then slid it against ripe, yielding flesh with a whisper of a sigh, cutting away a long strip that he let fall upon his plate, disregarded.

"Then," he said, "we strike."

CHAPTER THREE

The waiting was a lengthy business. The old king stubbornly clung to life, as though he imagined he could avert the discord that would follow his death. Red Rudolf made no effort to pay court to Flavia, I suppose because he was used to women being there for the taking, perhaps because he was a fool. He simply let it be known that he expected her to marry him, and a party in the Senate pushed for an early wedding to "settle him down." Flavia had none of it, and since she was a princess of the Blood, only the king could oblige her to obey.

A school of thought among the duke's partisans argued that Michael should set himself to overcome her obvious dislike and secure her hand under Rudolf's nose. I have never known a man to win an unwilling woman's heart by persisting against her wishes, and indeed, I have been paid a few times to make that point to suitors who wouldn't take no for an answer. Some men need that lesson hammered into their heads, sometimes literally. Michael refrained from the attempt. He said his interest would serve only to spur Rudolf's and he did not wish to bring the matter to a crisis. That was doubtless true, although one might also observe that Michael did not like to lose, or to be seen to lose, so much that he would rather not fight than risk failure.

And there was also the matter of de Mauban.

Antoinette de Mauban was a strikingly lovely woman in her early thirties, graceful, sensual, and charming. She had been the mistress of the Duke of Strelsau for four years, and Michael's attitude to her was a mixture of a man to his dog, and a dog to his bone. He was proud to display her, as any man of conventional tastes would be. He ran no risk of his carefully crafted public face by having her reign as his acknowledged mistress in Zenda. There was considered to be no shame in a man keeping a mistress; the populace applauded him because she was beautiful, and monklike virtue rarely wins hearts. He was intensely possessive, too, flying into a rage if reminded of the existence of her previous protectors. He didn't love her, but he took pleasure in owning her, and own her he undoubtedly did, body and soul. That much was made clear to me on the first occasion I encountered her, three weeks into my stay in Zenda, once she returned from a lengthy trip away.

I was summoned to Michael's private chambers on the first floor of the chateau. The drawing room I entered was a most elegant affair of drapes and gilt and marble, all white and gold like a church. Michael, in his habitual black, stood against it like a stain, and on the couch sat a remarkably beautiful woman, dark of complexion, dressed in the latest Parisian fashions. She gave me a blank look and an incline of her lovely neck. I gave her a blank look and a bow.

"Detchard," Michael said. "This is Mademoiselle de Mauban. My mistress. Detchard, my dear, is my new killer, and your new bodyguard."

Her eyes widened. "Michael—"

"I think you need one, don't you, my dear?" he said, with a lash in his voice. "And, to avoid any embarrassment, you should know that Detchard would be entirely resistant to your charms. He has no interest in female blandishments, isn't that right, Detchard? It must be a great freedom to you not to be enslaved to the wiles of womankind."

I cast about for an answer and settled for, "Your Grace."

"You will ensure that Mademoiselle de Mauban passes freely without molestation. I do not wish her to be bothered by importunate men, say, or unwanted friends, or persistent servants. And never by such things as secret letters and passed notes. That is beneath my mistress, and Detchard will ensure you are spared all that, my dear."

"Thank you, Michael," de Mauban said tonelessly.

"If you wish to walk or ride, he will accompany you—unless I have other use for him, in which case you will simply have to stay inside. I trust that's clear enough?"

"Yes, Your Grace," I said, and "Yes, my dear," she said.

Michael smiled. "Beautiful, isn't she?" he asked me, as though she were not there.

"Very."

"But wilful. A woman is like a horse: she must be broken before she will bear you as you need. Antoinette is mine alone, her affections only for me, and I wish her guarded until I can trust her to remember that."

"It would help to know what you want her guarded from," I said. "Someone else, or herself?"

His lips pressed white a second, and then he laughed. "Oh, you plain-speaking English. Antoinette adores me—don't you, my dear?—and yet she must needs struggle against her bonds. I have, shall we say, a hold over her, which she would remove if she could. I don't choose for her to do so, and she has been a little naughty in trying. A little disobedient, a little deceitful." He spoke playfully, as though recounting a shared jest. "So you will act for me, Detchard, and if anyone should be fool enough to attempt private communication, you will hurt them. Badly. I think even the most faithful of servants would be put off by a broken arm, don't you?" De Mauban shot a swift glance at me. Michael inclined his head, as though answering a question. "Indeed. Don't underestimate Detchard, my dear. He is a notorious man, and I should hate to see you weeping over the consequences of disobedience. There, now; I think all is clear. I hope you will get along."

I bowed again and withdrew, and took an exceedingly long breath as I stepped outside that gilded cage.

It was a couple of days before I was called upon to escort my new charge. The weather had been bad, confining us all to the chateau or the Tower, but at last the howling winds dropped. Michael was busy with ducal responsibilities, and a servant was sent to inform me that Mademoiselle wished my attendance.

She wore furs that looked like ermine, but sturdy boots. "I should like to walk," she said coldly. "And since I may not go without you, you must come with me."

"As mademoiselle wishes," I said, and fetched my own warm things.

I accompanied her out into the grounds. They were not extensive, since Zenda is hilly, but big enough that one could take a path well away from the castle, and see clearly in every direction of the snowy, empty landscape. There was not another soul out there, and though we could be seen for miles, we could not be heard.

We walked a few moments in silence, until at last my lady said, "You may as well speak."

"Jesus Christ," I said. "Toni. What the devil have you got yourself into now?"

"The devil is right. The absolute rotten-hearted shit. The son of a bitch. I hate him, I hate him so much. *Christ*, I hate him, the motherfucking shit-eating utter God-damned horse's arse. Thank you for coming, by the way," she added. "I didn't even know if you'd got the message. I've spent the last month wondering if I'd see you, or if it would be some other thick-necked brute, or if Michael had found out what I'd done and was going to torture me over it for Christ knows how long. God, I was glad to see you walk in."

"How long did it take you to set this up?"

"Months," she said bitterly. "Bloody months."

I had had the message back in Dresden from a mutual friend in the Berlin police, telling me that I would be approached for a job by a grand gentleman and that Toni Mauban begged me to accept the work "in the name of Paris." She didn't have to add that I owed her for saving my neck from the guillotine there; we both knew it. I'd sent back the message that I was at her disposal but heard nothing more, and had spent the last weeks in Ruritania kicking my heels and wondering why I was at the beck and call of a half-mad grandee in a tinpot country.

"I suppose you supplied him with all the information he had on me?" I enquired. "I ask purely out of interest, since he could quite easily have me hanged with what he knows."

"Franz arranged it," she said, naming our Berlin acquaintance. "I had to stay out of the business. Michael would never have allowed a friend of mine into the chateau—you would scarcely have been permitted into the country."

"He seems to be somewhat possessive," I agreed. "Shall I cut his throat for you?"

"God, yes. No, not yet," she amended. "You can't for now. Eventually, please do."

"And before then, can you tell me what's going on?"

The tale that emerged was a sorry one, and all too familiar, and it boiled down to one schoolgirl mistake. Toni Mauban—professionally the grande horizontale Antoinette de Mauban—had encountered Michael Elphberg in a salon several years back, and fallen deeply and passionately in love.

"Stupid," she said. "Stupid. I can't believe it now; it seems like a dream. *Love*, for God's sake. And yet I did."

"I can't see the attraction."

"I couldn't see the attraction when you were running all over town for that en travestie singer. How much did that affair cost you?" she sniped.

"Not as much as this has cost you, apparently."

She glared at me, and then her shoulders dropped. "Too true. There's no sense to it, is there? And Michael can be charming, utterly. He was fascinating, he didn't fall at my feet, but he watched me, and I . . . It's ridiculous. I haven't loved since I was sixteen. I thought I had learned my lesson then; I wish I had. Twice now I have destroyed my own life, and for what? Love. *Love*. There's a reason tennis players use that when they mean to say 'nothing.' Christ, I'm a fool."

"Amantes sunt amentes," I observed.

"What?"

"Lovers are deranged. Latin."

"Shove your classical education up your arse. Anyway, I fell in love with him. And that was my mistake."

She spilled it out, in far more detail than I needed, talking with the urgency of someone who had been too long silenced. She had loved him as he swept her away from the demi-monde and installed her with all honour as mistress of his Zenda chateau and Strelsau townhouse. She had loved him enough that it made her vulnerable, and slowly, as it so often does, the balance had shifted.

"I can't put my finger on it," she said, pacing on. "When the charm started to wear thin, when he began to order instead of ask, when I realised I was striving to please him and fearful I wouldn't and that nothing I could do was enough."

She had kept loving him, though, not with the practised passion of the courtesan, nor with the whole-hearted love of a woman who has found her mate, but with a passion that both fed and sickened her, like opium hunger. She loved him, and hated to love him, and hated herself for doing so. She had gone from commanding men's adoration to being the one who adored, and that was a fall she found very hard to stomach. And then she had fallen prey to the great curse of women's nature.

"I carried his child," she said. "He resented it, said my belly spoiled my beauty, but I had the baby. A girl. Her name is Lisl, and she changed everything. I loved her. Not when she emerged, all sticky and squalling and wrinkled—have you ever seen a newborn?"

"I have not."

"They're revolting. And the whole thing hurt dreadfully, and I dare say you don't want details, but the birth—"

"I don't want details."

"But it was worth it," Toni said softly. "Not at once, not for several days. But I held her, and her hands, so tiny, they clutched at me, and— I can't describe it. Something changed, inside me. Do you know those pictures, when you look at a black vase on a white paper and suddenly see two white faces against blackness? Like that. Everything shifted. I held her, and I felt myself loving her, and I looked at Michael, and he was like some poor paper cut-out of a man. He meant nothing to me any more, and I wanted none of him. I just wanted my daughter. He would have liked a son, you know; he looked down at her and said, quite casually, 'No use to me, then,' and I was so glad when he said that because I thought he'd let us leave." She took a deep breath. "So I told him that I wanted to take her and go. It was a stupid thing to do, but everything seemed so very simple and clear. I would go away with my daughter and never see him again, and everything would be perfect. I didn't *think*."

"I take it he didn't respond well to your request."

"Michael cannot bear to be left," she said. "He must be duke of our hearts, centre of the world, and if you let him know he's not, you might as well slap him in the face. He's spent his life being a poor second to his brother, and it makes him sick with rage. He won't have married servants, you know, because everyone in his service must put him first. That's why there are no women living here, to avoid affairs."

"Some of us don't need women to have affairs."

"He wouldn't like that any better, believe me. It is Michael first, last, and always. I *knew* that. I should have thought, and slipped away, but all I could think of was Lisl. So, yes. I told him I wanted to leave, and he took it poorly."

"Where is your daughter now?" I asked, and it was one of the harder questions I have ever asked, because I feared the answer.

"I don't know." Toni's face crumpled in a way I had never seen before. She looked small and fragile, and I wanted to hold her but could not risk it for fear we would be seen, and I scratched a long, deep mark on Michael's tally for that. "I don't *know*, Jasper. He took her away. I'm allowed to see her every couple of months if I behave, but never here. We meet in different locations every time, and she has a new nurse, a new set of men with her, so I can't make friends and it's not worth their while to help me. I tried bribing them last time and they reported back to Michael. That's why you are set to guard me, because I have been trying to find her. She's one and a half now, and I don't know where she's kept, and if I leave him I'll never find out—and I'm afraid."

"Of what?"

"He'll hurt her if I leave him," Toni whispered. "He said he would."

"His own child?"

"He doesn't care, she's just another Elphberg bastard. He says things—he'll scar her face, or he'll sell her to a brothel so she can grow up like her mother. Maybe it's only threats, but I can't take the risk. He's as mad as Rudolf, or as evil, whichever it is; he just hides it better. Oh God, what have I done?"

Made a bloody mess of things, it sounded like, but I was hardly the man to rebuke her for that. "So I'm here to find her?"

"I don't know what you can do. I'm exhausted, Jasper. If I only had myself to consider I could cope, but my daughter— I can't do this alone any more." Her voice cracked. I knew that note; one often hears it in people who have endured too much when help finally seems to be at hand. The prospect of a burden lifting does tend to make one aware of quite how heavy it is.

But it wasn't lifted yet, and this was no time for tears. "Well, you don't have to, so pull yourself together," I said briskly. "Come, Toni, act the woman. What is it you want?"

She shot me a lethal glare, set her lips as she composed herself, then said, quite clearly, "I want my daughter back, and then I want Michael Elphberg fucking dead."

"Noted," I said. "Perhaps somewhat on the challenging side, since he's a royal duke with a set of heavily armed henchmen, but I'll see what can be arranged. Who knows where Lisl is kept?"

"Nobody else in the castle, I'm sure of that. He sends instructions directly to someone, but I don't know who. I tried to bribe a servant, and he found out; I set my maid to search for me, and he dismissed her. He spies. The whole house is full of spies. He trusts nobody, because nobody can possibly love him enough for his liking."

"Have you tried going through his desk?" I took her withering look as a yes. "And do you believe she's safe for the moment?"

She nodded. "I have just come back from a visit. She's beautiful. She didn't know me, but she's beautiful."

"Then we're not on an urgent deadline. All right. If nothing else, I'll see if I can accompany you to your next meeting. When will that be, three months? Then I have time to ingratiate myself, to search, to see what the hell I can do. In the meantime, hold tight, don't provoke him, and keep smiling. Remember our agreement at the old place, the division of labour?"

She grinned at that. The duke's mistress Antoinette de Mauban was all elegant grace, but my old partner in crime Toni had a grin so filthy it brought men to their knees. "'I'll smile at them, you stab them.' Thank you, Jasper. God, it's good to have a friend here at last."

CHAPTER FOUR

We had to tread carefully. Toni was a bright woman, and Michael knew it; he in turn was no fool, and he had no intention of making it easy for her to escape. He wanted her broken to his will until she would obey his every whim because nothing else seemed possible any more. In the end he would not even have to restrict her movements or hold a threat over her head, because he would have put fetters on her soul. I did not delude myself that Toni was too strong for him, strong though she was; anyone can be broken if you go about it the right way.

We had two advantages: she was not broken yet, and he didn't know that she and I were friends. The second was a fragile strength, since all it would take would be a single slip, or a casual mention from Franz, his German police contact, that Toni had had him put my name forwards in the first place. Well, I had worked under greater threats than that, and if push came to shove, I intended to shove back with a blade.

I was coldly respectful to Toni in public, and she treated me as she did the others, with quiet dignity and reserve. Meanwhile, I worked hard to make myself invaluable to Michael. The easiest way out of this would be to make myself his trusted lieutenant. If he sent me to accompany Antoinette when next she was permitted to see the child, we could simply take Lisl and walk away over whatever bodies might be necessary. It would take time to manoeuvre myself into that role, but we had time, and it seemed to me safer than torturing the information out of Michael. He was a duke, and a stubborn bastard, and it hardly ever works anyway.

Winter lingered like an unwanted policeman for endless monotonous weeks, and then departed overnight. We woke one day to green meadows dotted with the beginnings of flowers, as the entire country seemed to throw off its blankets and burst into life at once. Birds sang, lambs appeared from nowhere, the peace of the Castle of Zenda was shattered, and my existence became thirty times as complicated. For the latter two facts, as for so many things, I can only blame Rupert of Hentzau.

My God, how to convey Hentzau on the page? One could not do it honestly without contravening the Obscene Publications Act. *A handsome villain*, Rassendyll calls him, *who feared neither man nor devil*. He was not yet twenty-three, with an impossibly fresh youthfulness to his face. His hair was thick and dark, his eyes darker and full of dancing demons. His upper lip had a curl to it that could be sneer or snarl or smile, or all of them, and he was in superb condition, trim, light-muscled, an athlete, a fencer, a rider most of all. I saw him first on horseback, trotting up the long broad avenue to the chateau one fine spring morning, and I will freely admit my mouth went dry.

I was taking the air with Toni in the grounds as the rider approached. I looked, and I may have stopped in my tracks to do it, because she gave me a dig in the side. "Cheri, you are not listening to me."

"Of course I am."

"No, you are not. You are—" She followed my gaze to the man approaching us. He rode a roan mare, a wonderfully elegant piece, but who could give a damn for horseflesh given the man-flesh atop it?

"Oh Jasper," she said. "Not him. *No.*"

"You know him? Who is he?"

The rider drew level and halted his horse. "Mademoiselle de Mauban!" he cried, lifting his hat and saluting her with a flourish so deep as to seem satirical. There was a feather in his hat, of course. He wore inadvisably tight trousers that hugged his well-muscled thighs, and a jacket of military cut, revealing just enough of his taut arse that I felt a strong curiosity to see more.

Toni inclined her head. The rider turned to me. "Greetings, sir." His smile was mocking, blinding. "Rupert of Hentzau, at your service."

"Jasper Detchard."

"Ah," he said. "I know your name. I am summoned to appear in His Grace's presence no later than eleven o'clock at my peril"—it had recently chimed noon—"but that duty done, I shall pay my respects with due ceremony and apology." His dark gaze flickered over me. "It will be a pleasure," he added, and clapped his heels to his horse.

I let out a long breath. Toni let out a groan. "*Jasper.*"

"Why not?" I enquired. "He looks game."

"For anything," she retorted somewhat tartly. "Hentzau is a rascal of the first order. Trouble in shining boots. Stay away from him, truly; we have enough on our plates. He is worse than he is handsome."

"I find it hard to believe that he is more anything than he is handsome."

"Well, he is. Really, you must not. It will not end well."

I swept her a bow. "But my dear mademoiselle, when do I ever choose courses that end well?"

She laughed a little at that. "Too true. But believe me, Hentzau will be the pinnacle of your poor decisions. They say he broke his mother's heart with his wildness," she offered, in a faux-moralising tone.

"Then he and I have something in common already. May I infer that we have tastes in common too?"

"I have heard he romances men and women alike. Some say simultaneously," she added with a sideways look.

"How intriguing."

"He is that, yes. And charming, handsome, pretty-mannered. But I don't hear that he's kind."

"Not being a maid in search of security, I don't seek kindness," I observed.

She was silent for a few seconds. When she spoke, she looked away from me. "I wish you would. I never thought of kindness, not really, until I was made to feel its lack. To love someone who is unkind . . ." She left that there, staring up the broad avenue at the gracious chateau, our master's domain. "Well. Anyway, Hentzau is a pretty piece, I grant you, but he is trouble to the bone. He is one of those men who has no heart."

"Then we will get on."

"Oh, don't be ridiculous. You have plenty of heart, just no soul."

"Thank you for your good opinion. But why do you imagine Hentzau's heart interests me in the slightest? The rest of his anatomy would do me very well indeed."

She exhaled. "It is your choice, dear Jasper. I wish you fortune, so long as that unreliable little sod doesn't get in our way. Go forth and conquer—or be conquered, as you prefer—and enjoy the ride."

Michael and his visitor were closeted together for some hours. I possessed my soul (if I have one) in patience for a while, became bored, and invited Lauengram to a bout with the foils. He was not my match, but a good swordsman nonetheless, and we gave each other a testing time up and down the practice court. It was a hot afternoon, unseasonably so, and we had both stripped to our shirtsleeves by the time we stopped for a cooling draught.

Lauengram took a long swig. "That's better. His Grace's kitchen brews an excellent ale."

"He is well served in all things," I agreed. "Who is it who serves him now? Some young sprig I saw riding up the great approach."

"Hentzau." Lauengram wiped his hand across his moustaches as though that was all he need say.

"And who is that when he's at home?"

"Oh, a little devil of the minor nobility. Flaunted his mistresses in his mother's house—a godly woman, on her sickbed—and drove her to her grave by it. He has killed his man in a duel, and cut throats in the street too. Drinking, gambling, wenching—and more than wenching, I hear," he added with a sideways look at me.

"He sounds a disreputable visitor for the sober Duke of Strelsau."

Lauengram gave his sharp bark of a laugh. "Oh, the worst of reputations."

"Then what is he doing here?"

"That I cannot say, but Hentzau has notoriously enjoyed Prince Rudolf's hospitality in Strelsau for the last few months. Drunken talk, public dissipation—and believe me, if Hentzau is involved, it is always public; he has no discretion. Perhaps he has something to say to

Duke Michael on Red Rudolf's behalf. Or perhaps he acts on our duke's command. Perhaps it is a taunt. I dare say we will learn."

We took up the foils again after we had drunk our fill. The practice ground was in a courtyard overlooked on all sides which rapidly trapped the sun's heat, and after another few brisk bouts I was sweating like a horse. There was a barrel of water in the corner of the ground, and I went over, scooped out a ladleful, and tipped it over my head, soaking the thin linen of my shirt and washing the heat from my scalp. The sensation was delightful. I added another couple of ladles, then splashed my face with a double handful of the cool water, shutting my eyes to enjoy the soaking.

"Good God," said a light, taunting voice. "What a fascinating display."

I shook my wet hair and blinked water from my eyes. There he stood in the doorway to the courtyard: Rupert of Hentzau, dark hair glistening in the sunlight, lips curving, eyeing me with an appreciation that struck me as excessively frank given Lauengram was standing there with us. *No laws here*, I reminded myself: not in Ruritania, and certainly not for Michael's man in Michael's stronghold.

I was aware that water ran in rivulets over my shoulders; that my shirt was soaked and, being fine linen, doubtless interestingly translucent; that I was somewhat sweaty and flushed, with my muscles corded from exertion. I dare say I looked well enough. I had ten years on him—thirteen, if I must be tediously accurate—but sun, campaigning, and late nights in smoky rooms had lined my face, while his was so youthful he looked the boy everyone called him.

Youthful, but not innocent. Not that at all.

He was looking me over, taking his time, a leisurely survey that disturbed me in a way I could not quite place, until I realised its meaning: he was looking at me as a man looks at a woman he is not obliged to respect.

Now, I am happy to be admired, and will gladly joust with heated glances until one may get down to business, but that was not how he looked at me. I can put it no better than to say, some men's looks give the message, *Shall we?* whereas Hentzau's insolent survey said, all too clearly, *Shall I?* with no interest in asking my opinion. He was considering if I merited his attention—I, Jasper Detchard, who had fucked and fought my way across two continents while this little shit preened himself in some spotty mirror—and the damned gall of it struck me very forcibly indeed.

"And do you only stand on the sidelines?" I asked.

"Oh, I like to play. If a partner merits my attention. I wonder if you might."

"Find out," I said, and I threw my foil at him. Perhaps rather hard, and rather suddenly, aimed at his face, and he flinched away even as his hand came out for it. A visible flinch, and he knew it, and sudden fury dawned on his handsome features.

Lauengram gave a cough of laughter and tossed me his foil, which I caught neatly, flicking the tip through the air with a satisfying hiss. "Go on, Detchard. Be cautious, Hentzau, if you can; you have met your master."

"Oh, we shall see about that." He put the foil down to strip off his tight coat and waistcoat, down to his shirt. I took the opportunity to run my eyes—insolently—over his form. A smooth man, agile, tautly and tightly muscled with a dancer's grace. Annoyance in his first movements, brought under control quickly but not quite quickly enough. Hentzau's temper might well be his weakness, I decided.

His form was excellent as he came to face me on the practice ground. The blunted tips of the foils whipped up in perfunctory salute, and we fought.

It is an interesting exercise to fight a man when neither of you is attempting to kill the other. Indeed, it is much like the distinction between a fuck that will be the first of many, and a hurried encounter without names or faces. When one does not have to rush to completion for one's own safety, one can take time to learn, to test, to probe weaknesses and explore peculiarities. The delicious pleasures of advance and retreat, the dance of feints and rushes, the finding of a rhythm that builds in speed and confidence, harder and faster amid the panting of harsh breath to the final thrust—

I seem to be digressing.

Hentzau was fresh where I was already heated, his reactions swift and sure. He was a good fencer, too: athletic in movement, light and swift, his foil flashing in the sun, and a taunting smile on those handsome, arrogant lips that were made to drive men to madness one way or another. I had to work hard in those few minutes to avoid being hit, and he forced me to a graceless twist and retreat that brought a quick pant of mocking laughter to his breath.

I was to see that again and again: Hentzau pricking and poking to drive his opponent into reckless anger. He struck at recklessness in other men because he knew it to be his own weakness, even while it won him prizes of which other men dared not dream.

It was a good strategy for most, but I am not reckless. Rassendyll somewhat patronisingly calls me *a cool man, relentless, but without Hentzau's dash*, and that is fair. Heroes are dashing. I prefer winning.

So I set myself to do it. I made a series of feints that forced him to turn until the sun was in his eyes; I used my superior reach and strength mercilessly, striking down the foil that leapt and darted at me with a heavy, joyless hand, knocking his blade out of the way rather than engaging in a test of skill. I could have danced with him to both our pleasure, but I was not here to please him. I wanted to win.

I could observe the growing annoyance on his face, since he had seen me fight far more gracefully with Lauengram. I was insulting his swordplay with my bludgeoning tactics, and he knew it, and was, I hoped, doubly enraged since he could not break through my guard to punish my insolence.

At last he made a daring move, what fencers call a flaconade, his blade circling mine and sliding along it with a rasp of steel to bend my foil out of the way even as he lunged. It was a perfectly executed attack that should, if there were any justice, have gone straight to my heart.

There is no justice, and I am too well acquainted with the showy devices of fencing-masters to be caught by such a thing. I twisted aside from his attack, disengaging my blade as I ducked low to the ground and braced myself with my free hand. It was a perfect passata sotto, if we are to talk of showy Paris-salon manoeuvres, executed with all the artistry I had denied him earlier, and I had then only to straighten my sword arm to tap his chest. I could have hit him hard enough to leave a bruise, but I judged the controlled touch would be more exasperating, and his expression showed that I was right.

"A fine bout," Lauengram said, applauding with a few slow, ironic claps as I rose.

"Another round," said Hentzau through his teeth.

"Hardly." That was a voice from the doorway, and I turned to see Michael standing there, watching. "Detchard, with me. Hentzau, I feel sure I gave certain instructions."

To give the devil his due, Hentzau showed no discomposure at that rebuke. He swept a dashing bow—naturally—and murmured, "Your Grace." Michael surveyed him with an assessing eye, and stood in the doorway waiting for me as I splashed my face and found my coat.

We climbed the Tower—several steep flights, punishing to overworked legs; I assumed that was deliberate—and walked along the ancient battlements, looking over the little town's red rooftops, and the rolling forests of Zenda that surrounded us, rising up the mountain slopes. Michael was silent for a while. Finally he said, "That was hard fought."

"He's a good swordsman."

"Oh, you are without question his master," Michael said dismissively. "He will have to trick you to beat you. I have no doubt he will."

"Your Grace is most flattering."

"He is to join us."

"Hentzau? Join the Five?"

"Now the Six. Indeed."

"I understood his reputation was of the worst," I offered cautiously.

"It is. He has partnered my brother in debaucheries which would be a matter of great scandal were they widely known." Michael's lips curved in a cold smile.

Rudolf the Red would doubtless soon learn his playmate had gone over to his brother's side. That would be a daily torture to a man who feared for his reputation, assuming Rudolf had the sense to do so, which I doubted. "I see."

"Hentzau will behave himself in my service," Michael added. "Or, at least, he will not make himself notorious in public. That is the subject on which I wished to speak to you, Detchard."

"Am I to be his keeper also?" I enquired, and received a chilling look.

"You will keep him from Mademoiselle de Mauban. He is a man who aspires to forbidden fruit."

"He would be brave to do so when it is Your Grace who forbids it."

Michael clasped his hands behind his back, walking the stone flags with a sure stride. "Hentzau wishes to join my party because he well knows the faction of the Red would not tolerate him. If or when my brother becomes king, wiser counsellors will see his playmates quietly removed, to avoid staining the dignity of the crown."

"They don't do that now," I observed.

"Rudolf would only find new playmates. There is no point trying to restrain him until he is king."

"But will he not choose his own companions then?"

"He will quickly be fettered to my cousin the Snow Queen. I imagine she will freeze his hot blood." His voice rang with repressed rage. Evidently he resented Flavia's refusals. "In any case, Hentzau has now chosen his side—or so he says."

"You doubt him, sir?"

"I doubt everyone," Michael said. "You will watch Mademoiselle de Mauban for me, and you will watch Hentzau too and satisfy yourself of his faithfulness. Do not set yourself up as his enemy; I don't want him to feel he is suspected. And he is an able man. He may be of great use to me. But I wish to be sure, and you will make sure for me."

"With pleasure, Your Grace."

"But, Detchard? Hentzau has . . . charm." Michael pronounced the word with disdain, having no great interest in talents he lacked. "You will not be charmed."

"It is not my habit, Your Grace."

Michael turned abruptly, fixing me with his compelling glare. "Mark me well. I will not have you tumbling into bed with Hentzau. You owe your loyalty, your devotion, to *me*. Do you understand?"

"Entirely, sir." I had seen the truth of Antoinette's words for myself. Michael was as jealous as a child, ever demanding to be first in the hearts of everyone around him, enraged beyond measure at the idea that he was not the centre of all our worlds. He would never let Antoinette go, simply because she dared to wish to leave him; I had no doubt he had removed her daughter in part because he feared the rivalry of a baby. "Your Grace, I am not here for diversions. I prefer work to play. And pretty boys are ten a penny." I bowed my knee to him, lowering my head. "I have greater ambitions."

He nodded, a flush of pleasure on his cheeks. "Good. You are a loyal servant, Detchard. But we both know men are weak, so make use of Krafstein's skills. It's what he's there for. Perhaps Hentzau's intentions are honest, but if they are not— Well, he now knows he can only beat you by trickery or treachery. Be watchful. Be wise. And do not be seduced. That is an order."

CHAPTER FIVE

I am nothing if not obedient. Michael had ordered me to watch Hentzau, and I did. I watched his walk, the movement of his graceful frame, and the way he smiled, which was an offence to decent citizens in its blend of mockery and invitation.

He mocked continually, as though he lived in a permanent state of amusement with the world, and if Michael had not forbidden serious duelling, I think he would have found himself in grave trouble with at least three of our company. Only to Michael did he speak with courtesy untainted by irony; often he forgot even with Michael, which suggested either courage or foolhardiness. The rest of us were left with the sensation of being continually ridiculed. One could not entirely blame him, since Krafstein and the Belgian were both ridiculous in their vile way; and Hentzau's endless rhapsodies on de Gautet's ridiculous facial hair were very funny indeed. He composed an Ode to Monsieur's Waxed Moustache one evening and declaimed it at the dinner table, and I never saw Michael laugh so hard as then, all ambition and resentment briefly forgotten. We all roared, even the usually humourless de Gautet, and that evening we were not the Duke of Strelsau and his six henchmen, but a party of seven companions, fellows in mirth.

The fact was, Hentzau could bring life to a funeral home. He had so much of it, that merry young villain. He flirted with Antoinette just a trifle past what was permissible, and brought a real, if reluctant, smile to lips that were too often held tightly against sorrow. He trailed innuendo past me, every speech hiding a challenge under the laughter.

I watched him. He watched me.

The first weeks passed without incident, or at least without anything that developed into an incident. It was noticeable that Hentzau kept an eye on Antoinette, as though he wished to find her alone. I made myself her constant companion—I had Michael's orders, plus a very fair idea of the chivalry of the Ruritanian nobleman towards any lone woman. Since Hentzau was not in the slightest discouraged by my impersonation of a bulldog, the three of us spent a certain amount of time together, which caused me and Antoinette to curse his name, since it meant we could not speak freely. He smiled at me, and I at him, and we both made light conversation and waited for the other to go. He flitted between German, French, and English with as much ease as Antoinette or I.

"So tell me," he remarked one day as we walked in the chateau's small but elegant grounds. "How does a proper English gentleman become a blade for hire?"

"I don't know. Perhaps you should ask one."

He laughed. "Please, Detchard. You are as proper as any Englishman alive—in soul."

"I struggle to see how you reach that conclusion from my history," I observed, finding myself really quite annoyed. I had not lived the life I had to be called *proper*. "And I am reliably informed I lack a soul."

He waved a hand. "To be removed from schools is nothing. You did very well in the British Army, I believe." I snorted. "Were it not for the cards and the men, I grant you. I understand you have a taste for privates?"

"I think I see His Grace approaching," Antoinette said, with just the right tone of cultured disgust, and removed herself from our company, probably to howl with laughter.

"For God's sake, Hentzau," I said. "She is a lady."

"She's a courtesan."

"She is still a lady."

"What nonsense is this? You will cut throats in back alleys but not tolerate a ripe jest in front of a woman who is all ripeness? You can't imagine there's anything you can teach her about men's peculiarities."

"There are still conventions to be observed."

"There you have it: proper," he said triumphantly. "Had you been born with two thousand pounds a year and an inclination for the fair sex, I dare say you would never have broken a law in your life. *Do* you incline to the fair sex, ever? I suppose not or Michael would not have set you as the dragon to guard his treasure."

"I cannot see it is any of your damned business."

"Spoilsport. You could let me alone with her, you know."

"No, I could not."

"I could persuade you? I am extremely persuasive."

I replied to that in language more suited to a barracks than a chateau. He only laughed. "I mean her no harm, dogged Detchard."

"I don't give a damn what you mean. Stay away from her."

"Five minutes' private conversation. You may keep a watchful eye from a distance if you like."

"Let me make this clear: if you bother Mademoiselle de Mauban, I will kick you twice round the Tower. Do we understand one another?"

"As I said, proper," he repeated, apparently unimpressed.

"Proper or not, we both know who would win a fight," I said, feeling by now somewhat provoked.

He gave me an assessing look, one without the usual salaciousness. "Could we have a practice bout, you and I?"

"I thought one was enough for you."

"Not at all. You are my better with the blade, I admit it freely, in skill but also in your tactics. I should like to take advantage of that. I hardly ever meet anyone I consider my better," he explained, and there was a kind of purity in that arrogance that took my breath away.

"Michael has bidden me not to fight you." It was a weak response, and the tilt of his brow told me he thought the same.

"Really? Come, Detchard. Surely a practice bout—"

"Our last practice bout was not amicable. Do you imagine the next will be better?"

He lowered his long lashes, as dark and curled as any pretty girl's could be. "Perhaps not. I have the impression you don't like me, Englishman."

"I can't imagine why," I said, and left him.

A few days later Michael was obliged to attend to business in Strelsau. He took Lauengram and Krafstein as bodyguards, and Toni for his own reasons. De Gautet accompanied them in order to see a tailor, and that left Bersonin in his alchemical cell playing with poison, me, and Rupert of Hentzau.

Michael spoke to me before he left. "Keep an eye on Hentzau in my absence."

"Do you have any new grounds for your suspicions?" I asked. "Hentzau seems to me a shameless young hound, but I have seen no duplicity or ulterior motive yet. I think he's here for the adventure of it."

"Perhaps," Michael said. "But he rides to Zenda to post his letters. Letters to Strelsau."

He had not shared that with me before. I nodded. "He may be hiding the identity of a correspondent for a number of reasons, of course. And he takes any excuse to ride."

"Oh, I dare say he is a fine horseman," said Michael, who was not, in a dismissive tone. "Nevertheless—"

"I shall watch, Your Grace. Consider me your eyes and your right hand in this." Fulsome pledges do not come naturally to me, I may say, but they went down too well with the duke to be omitted.

Michael seemed satisfied. "Tell me what he does when I am not here; if he seeks to meet anyone in private. Tell me what he wants."

The party for Strelsau duly set off early in the morning. Bersonin hid himself away in the Tower at once; one of his few redeeming qualities was that he was as reluctant to have my company as I was to have his. I was alone in the chateau but for Hentzau.

My first instinct was to raid Michael's private rooms for papers. I restrained it, wanting to be sure I was unobserved. Moreover, even as Michael had tasked me to watch Hentzau, it would not have surprised me in the least to learn that he had tasked Hentzau to watch me—or put the servants on both of us, come to that. Michael Elphberg was not a trusting man.

I decided my best course was to be what I seemed: the loyal henchman. I therefore prowled the grounds, put in a couple of hours on the practice yard to keep myself in fighting trim, went for a ride around the duke's domain, and returned some way past noon with an appetite for my luncheon, to discover Hentzau in a padded silk dressing gown. Apparently, he had just got out of bed.

"You're an idle hound," I remarked, with the moral superiority of a man who has done his work for the day.

"You're excessively keen," he growled. "What are you running around for, with the duke absent? What's that thing you English say? When the cat's away, the mice will stay in bed as long as they choose."

"You won't improve your fighting skills that way," I pointed out. "Or any other."

He glowered at me. "What, precisely, is the point of getting yourself kicked out of the Army, taking up as a blade for hire, and then living like a monk? Why would I get up at reveille to train if I don't have to?"

"Because if you don't, you'll lose to the men who do. Youth only carries you so far, Hentzau; the rest is hard work."

"God, I dislike you," he said. "Will you give me that practice bout, then?"

"Only if you earn it. I'm not wasting my time on a bleary-eyed, bacon-stuffed layabout."

He paused in the act of lifting another forkful of bacon to his lips and gave me a look so full of affronted dignity that I could not help but laugh. "Very well. I shall ride off my breakfast—"

"Luncheon."

"—*breakfast*, and we could practice at, say, four o'clock?"

"You plan a long ride."

He shrugged negligently. "It appears to be a beautiful day, and as you have so elegantly hinted, I should benefit from a little healthful exercise."

I agreed to that, and we finished our meals in relative peace.

He did indeed set out on horseback once dressed. I watched him go from the top of the Tower. It had a commanding view of the area, and I had a telescope. I could track his progress a fair distance, and by the time I lost sight of him, I was quite sure that Hentzau's healthful exercise was taking him, not through any of the open countryside or pretty forest paths, but directly to Zenda town. *Interesting*, I thought, and wondered if Michael's suspicions had any ground.

We met in the practice yard that afternoon. Hentzau arrived a good fifteen minutes late, and looked warm, as though he had hurried. "I beg your pardon, Detchard. I rode longer than I thought."

"Where did you go?"

"Oh, up in the direction of Tarlenheim, along the bridle path that tops the hills. It's a good clear ride."

"Yes, a marvellous view. And it's pleasant to be out of the bustle of a town," I agreed experimentally.

"God, do you think so? I can't bear the silence of the countryside, it's like a flowery graveyard. And views are all very well but, you know, one can buy paintings for that. Give me town any day."

"Then you should go to the town."

"Dear fellow, I pray daily that Michael will take us all back to Strelsau," he assured me. "Shall we have that bout?"

I chewed over his words as we measured the foils. I knew the route to Tarlenheim of which he spoke, and he had not taken it; he had also avoided two clear opportunities to mention he had just been to, or near, Zenda town. I had no idea what he was up to, though I suspected it was no more than some illicit affair with the mayor's wife or daughter—or both, or indeed the mayor himself for all I cared. It scarcely mattered. To secure Michael's trust, I was quite ready to use Rupert of Hentzau's love life as a burnt offering.

We fought for a couple of hours, until the evening chill drew in and the light began to go. Hentzau put his mind and his back into it, and tested me sorely at a couple of points. That handsome face and the rakish posturing hid a powerful desire to excel, and I found myself enjoying the role of teacher with such a pupil.

When I think back to my months in Zenda, the memories that come most readily to mind are of those times on the practice yard. The setting sun catching the foils with golden kisses, the smell of dust and male sweat; feet scuffing on hard ground, harsh breaths, the hiss and scrape of blades and an occasional wordless shout of triumph. The sheer animal vitality of Rupert Hentzau, intolerably lovely in a loose white shirt with his throat bare, probing me for any weakness and smiling like a devil while he did it. And the constant aching pulse of my desire, throbbing in my belly like a burn that would not heal.

I had wanted him since I saw him, with a raw hunger that built by the day and whispered bitter temptation at night, and the unguarded physical pleasure of our sword-dance did nothing to dull the edge of that wanting. But desire is nothing; even a dog can be trained to control its urges. I needed to get to Antoinette's child, and that left no space for dalliance when Michael was such a jealous master.

The damned inconvenient, interfering, inbred son of a bitch. I added another mark to the tally against him, to be paid off in due course, agreed to another bout with Hentzau on the morrow, and strode off to sluice myself down with cold water in peace.

It was a frustrating time. I had hoped to get into Michael's private rooms in his absence. Toni had searched already, and she was faster, quieter, and more experienced than I (she had obliged the French government a few times while the Prussian ambassador was in her thrall), so I doubted I could find what she could not, but it was at least possible that Michael would keep the secret close only while she was present, and feel no reason to be so careful in her absence. But his apartments were well secured, with an excellent new lock on the strong door, and the windows were shuttered in his absence. I have never been able to acquire any facility at picking locks, and I knew that any attempt to force the door or break a window would be detected, if not in the act then certainly afterwards.

I wondered whether I could use Michael's suspicions and blame Hentzau for any intrusion, possibly cutting his throat first to prevent inconvenient denial, and decided against it as unlikely to convince; he wasn't a surreptitious-burglary sort of man. It is often possible to circumvent these problems with a payment to the servants, but I dared not, feeling sure that they would be quick to report back to our master. In fact I found myself in the position of Tantalus in every way, with my desires dangled temptingly in front of me, yet ever out of reach.

A night-time assault from the outside was the only option, I concluded. Windows above ground level rarely have the most secure fastenings, and shutters are often latched rather than locked. A piece of thin flexible metal can usually deal with that, and my larcenous skills certainly stretched so far. The only question was how well secured Michael's windows were, and I would need to get up to the first floor, from the outside, to find out.

I went that night, losing no time. Michael's party was supposed to be absent for a few days, but he was always erratic and Zenda was not a great distance from Strelsau. I waited until three in the morning, when the castle was silent and sleep is at its deepest. Bersonin was in the Tower that night. Michael's windows faced the moat and the ancient building, so I had to hope that he was asleep; I saw no glimmer of light from the narrow windows. Hentzau slept on the first floor, a few rooms away from Michael. He and Lauengram were lodged there while the rest of us had smaller quarters on the second floor, I suppose to make the point that Ruritanian nobles were superior to hired killers. It saved me trouble. I went cat-footed along the dark corridors from my room to find the staircase that led to the roof, and let myself out into the chilly spring night, working my way around the parapet to avoid tramping across a servant's ceiling. It is remarkable how heavy a tread on a roof can sound to a listener below.

I reached my goal, the edge of the roof above Michael's rooms, and tied my rope: a thin, strong piece of cord, dyed black, that could take my weight and more. There was a waxing moon, which gave plenty of light for my work. I lashed the cord firmly to the parapet, since nothing sturdier seemed available, testing the ornamental stone to be sure it was firmly fixed, and then I went over the edge and down.

It had been a while since I had climbed a rope, and my arms and shoulders protested vigorously. I took it slowly anyway, despite the temptation to slide down and relieve the strain, not wishing to risk making a noise. The castle grounds were not patrolled at night, so I should be safe if I kept my silence.

I wall-walked the last few yards (accidentally swinging into and smashing a window on this sort of job is a thing you only do once). Michael's window was of the French style, with narrow full-length glass doors and a balcony. I found the stone rail with my feet, lowered myself to stand on the balcony and let the strain recede from my arms. With my breath back, I set about trying the fastening of the shutters.

They were, to my satisfaction, latched rather than bolted from the inside, and after a few moments' work, I flipped the latch up with a *clack* that echoed in the silent night, and eased a shutter open. The room inside was pitch dark; I saw a vague shape of my own reflection in the glass-paned doors. I took out my metal strip, and set out to discover if I could coax the doors open.

A good fifteen minutes later I concluded I could not. I am aware that this rarely happens in exciting narratives of derring-do and adventure, but nevertheless it happened now, and if that failure exasperates the reader, imagine how I felt. Michael bolted his French doors securely at the top and bottom, and unless I broke several panes of glass, I would not get in.

I was wondering whether to try another window, which would involve either jumping the considerable distance to the next balcony or climbing up my rope and lowering it again several feet along, when I heard the scrape of a foot on dry ground.

I froze. There was little chance that any night-walker would fail to notice the open shutter revealing the dark window, since the chateau was built of pale stone and the shutters painted yellow, but my black-clad form might be invisible against the glass. Or it might not. I had a knife strapped to the small of my back, and if I could catch my observer I could cut his throat and throw him in the moat without trouble, but it was a long way down from the balcony to the ground, too far to jump. I would need to climb, and the watcher would have plenty of time to raise the alarm.

In that case I should have to run for it anyway, and therefore, perhaps I should kick in the window, search while I could, and fight my way out. Hentzau was the only worthwhile opposition in the castle at the moment, and he had drunk well at dinner; he would be slowed and sleepy.

Those thoughts came far more quickly than the words to tell them. I was just tensing myself to put a foot to the French doors when I heard another noise, even quieter. I turned this time, and just saw a shadow of movement as someone or something retreated round the corner of the chateau.

I shoved the shutters closed. There was no way to latch them from the outside, but that was too bad. I sprang for my rope and swarmed up it like a sailor, hauling myself up with arms and legs, ears straining for the shouts that would raise the chateau. None came. I made it to the top, panting, swung myself over the parapet, unlashed my cord, and went as fast as I dared over the roof without thundering. No point waking the house with my footsteps.

Still no sound. Had the observer not seen me? I could hardly believe it. Was he—or she—raising the alarm quietly, shaking shoulders and murmuring for help?

I had looped up my cord as I proceeded. I slipped the bundle into a pocket and gently opened the door that led back into the chateau. Every movement had to be whisper-silent now; I felt a strong urge to run, and reminded myself how foolish it would be.

I bolted the door to the roof and made my way down the pitch-black stairwell, into the corridor, which seemed almost bright in the moonlight coming through the windows. I slipped along in silence, increasingly reassured that nobody seemed to be making a fuss. Perhaps, after all, the noise had been made by an animal. I had not seen much more of the shape than movement; it could have been a boar or a wolf. And if it was a human, well, it seemed whoever it was did not feel inclined to alert the house. I might yet be safe.

I reached the turning into the corridor on which my room lay, rounded the corner, and came face-to-face with Rupert of Hentzau, standing in the open hall at half past three in the morning.

My approach had made no noise, a fact of which I could be sure because he recoiled in shock. That gave me time to conquer my first instinct, pull my hand away from the small of my back and the wicked little blade I kept there, and demand, "What are you doing?"

"What am *I* doing?" he repeated, with some astonishment. "What are *you* doing?"

I pushed him back. He wore a dressing gown which looked garish even with its colours flattened by moonlight. It was open almost to the waist, secured with a loosely tied belt, and he wore no nightshirt, so that his bare chest was visible to the navel. When I pushed him, my fingers met his skin. "There was a noise, outside," I said, keeping my voice low. "It sounded like an intruder. Did you hear it? Or was it you?"

"Oh, you're looking for an intruder?" he retorted. "I see you stopped to dress."

He had me there, without question. Our eyes locked in the moonlight. I still held my hand against his chest; I could feel the rise and fall of his breathing under my fingers.

"You would find yourself at a disadvantage fighting half-naked," I said, and the necessity of whispering made my words sound too breathy.

"But what a charming distraction I'd provide. Cold on the feet, though." I glanced down involuntarily, and saw that his feet were indeed bare, and dirtied too. He'd been outside.

I looked up again, moving my hand to my hip to put it near my knife, but Hentzau showed no intent to attack; he merely smiled. "You know, Detchard, you needn't make excuses to me."

"Excuses?" I repeated with all the incredulity I could summon.

"If you were pursuing your own interests, well, you're not the only one. A man has a right to go about his private affairs unmolested, doesn't he? Michael would have us all be joyless, but that doesn't suit me. So perhaps we could agree that your nocturnal activities are no more Michael's business than, let's say, my own excursions, hmm?"

It was as good as telling me, *You scratch my back, I'll scratch yours.* I would keep quiet about his trip to Zenda, and he wouldn't mention a disturbed night, and me fully dressed at three in the morning. I weighed up the odds and concluded I had no choice.

I stepped back, releasing him. My hand felt cool away from his chest. "As you say. Some matters are nobody else's business."

"I'm so glad we agree. I'd hate to fall out with you, dear Detchard." His eyes glittered dark. "And I hope your evening was fulfilling. I am for my bed now, unless you feel there might be any chance of unlawful entry tonight? I'd hate to miss the opportunity."

"I shouldn't think so," I said through my teeth.

"Then I trust we'll fight tomorrow."

"Do you know, Hentzau, I have absolutely no doubt we will."

CHAPTER SIX

My frustrated housebreaking went otherwise unnoticed. Michael's party returned in a couple of days, and I was forced to tell Antoinette I was no further forwards. I informed Michael that Hentzau had done nothing suspicious in his absence, and could only hope he would hold to our late-night accord.

I wasn't sure what he was about. I could not be positive that he had seen my attempted break-in. If he had, and chose to ignore that one of Michael's most trusted men had attempted to break into his rooms, that would raise a great number of questions about his own loyalty. Even if Hentzau believed I had been out on the fuck, his stipulation still meant that he knew Michael was having him watched, and that he did not want his movements reported back. In fact, the little sod was unquestionably up to something. But I did not accuse him, and he did not accuse me.

A few weeks passed. Hentzau did not ride alone again, and seemed every inch the loyal, if disrespectful, courtier. I watched him. He watched me back. Sometimes we fought, always with others around us; we did not speak privately.

Antoinette was permitted another visit to her daughter. I asked Michael if he would have me accompany her and was turned down flat.

"I am training my hawk to fly from my hand and return without jesses," he told me. "Antoinette may roam Europe as she chooses; she is not my prisoner."

"You no longer feel she needs watching?" I asked doubtfully.

"If she needed watching still, I should have failed. No. I have given her . . . inducements to behave. That will do, I think. She will travel alone."

That was his decree. I soon learned what the inducements were: Michael had announced, quite simply, that if she did not return on the date he had set, or if any effort was made to take the child or follow her keepers, she would never see Lisl again. It was, he told her, a test of her obedience. Antoinette made the journey to Munich alone, and only there was informed she had to go on to Paris to see her daughter. I had no contacts in Paris anyway, since I had not been able to set foot there for years; Antoinette did, but she did not dare use them. She believed Michael was looking for an excuse to punish her, and I imagine she was right. She was away a fortnight all told, dragged over the Continent then made to kick her heels in Paris and carry out errands for Michael, and, she told me later, she was only permitted to see Lisl for three days.

I did what I could in her absence, which was little enough. Michael handed all his correspondence to his loyal manservant Max; I considered waylaying the fellow and taking his postbag off him, but I doubted I could do that more than once, so the chance of a randomly chosen bag containing something useful was slim. I also endeavoured to ingratiate myself further with Michael so that he might hand the business over to me, but got nowhere. Michael preferred to torment her himself.

I attempted one of these conversations the morning before he set out for Strelsau. Letters had been flying back and forth, and I hoped to "take some work off his hands." Michael was in a truly foul mood that day, tense and irritable, and dismissed me discourteously enough that I went out for a walk to regain control of my temper. I strode the hills for several hours without achieving that aim, and was marching back up the drive when I heard a cheery cry and saw Hentzau hailing me.

"There you are, Detchard. I was looking for you. A bout with the blades?"

"No." I kept walking.

He caught up after a few steps. "You seem unusually grim. And considering that you're *usually* grim, that's saying something."

"I just want solitude."

"Oh, that's a pity," he said, setting himself to match my pace. "Lovely day, isn't it?"

It was beautiful weather, with spring shading into summer. The trees were in bright leaf, the meadows sweet with wild flowers, and the birds made their usual racket. "Appreciate it yourself," I said.

"I am, I am. Have you heard, the old king is on his last legs?"

"I have heard variations on that theme for months."

"They say he has spoken to the Senate, asked if he can give his blessing to Michael. They say he wishes to choose his successor. That's why Michael is heading for Strelsau now: he intends a last-ditch appeal to the Princess Flavia to accept his hand. He believes that their alliance would surely sway the King and Senate in his favour."

"I wish him luck."

"You may well. It's his last chance to do this honourably. If Rudolf is made king and marries the princess, Michael will be out in the cold for good."

"I dare say."

"I would expect you to be more distraught," he said with a sideways glance. "As Michael's loyal man."

"I would have expected you to be heading for Strelsau ready to help him woo the princess," I said. "As—as you say—his loyal man."

"I wasn't invited," Hentzau said with a grin. "I dare say he's afraid I'll snatch her royal heart from under his nose."

"I'm sure a princess of the Blood would raise her skirts at the first snap of your fingers."

"You'd think so, wouldn't you?" he agreed. "And yet when I met her, she seemed inexplicably unmoved by my charms. Perhaps she had a cold."

I couldn't help smiling. He was an arrogant rogue, but he could laugh at himself. "You should have tried harder."

"Clearly. I don't think I'm in the mood for red hair, though. You know how it is: some days one wants beefsteak, other days only the lightest pastry will do."

"Tell Flavia she doesn't suit your delicate palate," I suggested. "I'm sure it will go well."

"I can't help my feelings," Hentzau said soulfully. "Princesses mean nothing to me. I want— Do you want to know what I want?"

"No."

"Yes, I thought you would. I'm in a mood for blondes, I think."

"Really."

"Blondes and secrets. I find that fascinating: fair hair and dark motives. Does anyone like that spring to mind?"

I had wondered if he would raise the topic of that late-night meeting again; this was more blatant than I had expected, and I was not sure how to respond. I would have liked to believe it was simply an approach; I highly doubted that, but I decided to play the game as though it were. "Nobody available to you, no. I thought you had a paramour tucked away in the town?"

"Sir, you cast doubt on my good name. Come, Detchard, might we not be frank with one another?"

"Certainly," I said. "Michael has forbidden me to fuck you, but since I imagine that has deprived me of at most half an hour's mild entertainment—"

"Oh, now, that's just rude."

"—I am happy to obey him," I concluded. "So I'm afraid you will have to satisfy your longings elsewhere."

"And what about my curiosity?"

"You were practising your English idioms recently," I said. "Let me remind you that curiosity killed the cat. Good day."

"They say the people cry Michael's name in Strelsau," de Gautet observed that evening. Michael had taken his two respectable Ruritanians with him to the capital, the better to create an unflattering contrast to Prince Rudolf, who was being dragged back from the fleshpots of Berlin to his father's deathbed. We three foreigners and Hentzau were seated around the table with a bottle. Hentzau seemed to have taken my rebuff in good spirits; I wondered all the more what it was he wanted. "They say the city will rise for him."

"And will this 'they' take up a musket or a pitchfork?" I asked. "Colonel Sapt of the king's guard seems to be keeping Michael's supporters down with a heavy hand."

"If anyone rises it will be the republicans, not our party," Bersonin observed.

I felt a certain sympathy for anyone calling for an end to the Elphbergs, of whom I was becoming heartily sick, but Ruritania's republicans were a vile and fanatical crew. Their leader, Anders, announced as his aims the seizure of the royal lands and wealth for the common good, which was to say his own pocket, and the expulsion of all foreigners. His definition of that group included any citizen who had a non-Ruritanian parent or grandparent, and anyone, no matter how long settled here, who did not adhere to the Christian religion. "Anders is a prick," I said. "Michael had me attend a public meeting of his, and a nastier rabble I have rarely seen. Have you heard him speak? The man is a ranting demagogue."

"The duke should have him disposed of," Bersonin said. "It would only take a little powder in a cup of ale. A pinch or two, no more." He sounded rather wistful at the prospect.

"It would end this dissent," de Gautet agreed.

"The dissent could be ended by anointing a competent monarch, if King and Senate had the sense to choose one on anything but the colour of his hair," I said. It never hurt to remind people of my fervent loyalty to Michael. Hentzau leaned back and, unseen by the others, rolled his eyes.

De Gautet shook his head. "It would not work. You are too English, Detchard, too much in the habit of picking and choosing your kings."

"That's rich coming from a Frenchman."

He ignored me. "If the King and Senate may select the ruler, the people will ask themselves why they should not do the same, and they will ask loudly. There will be riots. The fact is, Rudolf is not fit to be king, Michael is not born to be king, and Flavia lacks the wherewithal to be king." He made an obscene gesture to convey the wherewithal that Flavia lacked. "The King and Senate will not dare to challenge tradition, because that is all that keeps the entire edifice from falling around their ears. Michael cannot become king while Rudolf lives. I am certain of it."

"There's only one solution to that," Bersonin said. "Would that the duke would take it."

The old king died two days later. He left Michael the castle and estate of Zenda outright, a generous share of the country's lands and wealth in a highly significant strategic position, but as de Gautet had predicted, he did not dare to hand away the crown. The prize, as was always destined, went to the Red Prince, now Rudolf V of Ruritania. Long live the king.

Michael summoned the nobles Hentzau and Lauengram to his side for the State funeral while the rest of us kicked our heels in Zenda. The ducal party returned a week later, in a flurry of black mourning weeds and blacker temper. I stood with Antoinette as we watched the carriages coming up the drive. Rupert Hentzau rode in front, his graceful form and the magnificent beast between his legs enough to mark him out at a distance. Antoinette was tense by my side.

Hentzau trotted up to the steps on which we stood, wheeling his horse and doffing his feathered hat like a chevalier. "Madame, monsieur. Greetings."

"How is he?" Antoinette asked without preamble.

"Terrible. I would suggest you get out of the way and do not appear till he has sent for you. You too, Detchard. He is ripe to murder. I am quite serious."

He had, I noted, a bruise on his cheekbone, marring the smooth beauty of his features. I lifted a finger to my own face. He gave me a sour smile. "Indeed. Be warned."

"I shall not," Antoinette said. "He will need someone by him. I shall not leave him now." She looked every inch the loyal lover. I could only applaud her acting skills.

"I really would," Hentzau said. "On your head be it, my lady, but I really, truly would. Come to the stables with me, Detchard."

"I think I'll stay," I said.

Hentzau shut his eyes in exasperation, then gave a laughing shrug. "On both your heads, then. À bientôt."

He trotted his horse away. We waited in silence for a few minutes as the slower conveyances drew up. A footman came to open the door of Michael's carriage and was sent stumbling back as the man inside emerged with a curse.

Michael had brooding features at the best of times; now the skin was drawn tight such that we saw the skull under the skin. His lips were white with pressure, and I could see a tic pulse in his throat. He stalked up the stairs without a word or a look, and I stepped instinctively back. Antoinette came forwards, hands out.

"Michael," she said, voice soft and aching with compassion. "My dear."

He turned to her. She did not recoil at the expression on his face, but reached out and put a loving hand on his forearm.

He swung his arm up violently, throwing off her hand, and then the back of his own hand cracked savagely against her cheek.

Antoinette gave a cry and staggered back, clutching her face. Michael took another pace forwards, hand still raised and fingers forming a fist, and I said, "Your Grace."

He did not acknowledge me, even look at me, but he lowered his hand and said in a tone of pure venom to the cowering woman, "There. You have what you wanted: my failure, my shame. Be satisfied, bitch."

He strode off. I offered Antoinette a hand, but she shook me off, saying in a muffled voice, "Don't," and hurried into the hall. I let out a long breath, and went looking for Hentzau.

He had evidently finished rubbing down his horse—careless though he was with human life, I never saw him ignore a horse's needs—and was standing outside the stable door stretching the kinks from his back as I approached. I was not in a mood to appreciate the view, as he seemed to glean from my face, for his first remark was (inevitably), "I told you so."

"He hit her," I said in English, for discretion.

"The bastard hit *me*."

"You deserve it. You ought to be kicked regularly."

"There's no point abusing me because you failed to do anything to him," Hentzau observed with annoying accuracy. "Come for a walk."

"I don't want to come for a walk."

"In that case, come and help me take these riding boots off."

I let him know, in no uncertain terms, that I was not his valet. He laughed at me. "Michael will be rendering the chateau a hellhole. Come and hide in the Tower."

I followed him out and round, towards the Tower. He chattered the whole way, as sunny as a schoolboy as he spoke of a dead king and a lord's hopes dashed. "There were crowds in the streets overnight, standing for the duke, some for the prince, many I think to bid the king farewell. It was, shall we say, unrestful. Much shouting in the distance, and constant rumours that something was happening two streets along, but the king's guard were out in force."

"What about Michael's people?"

"He had none," Hentzau said with breezy contempt. "I should have had agents fomenting a riot and shouting my name; he considered it too great a risk to rebel openly. The highest stake a man could play for, yet he would not wager. That's why he's so angry; he refused the fence and he knows it."

"If he had declared rebellion against the new king, there would be fighting in the streets now."

"So he should have struck before the prince became king."

"While his father was on his deathbed, you mean? Send him to his grave with the sound of his sons' civil war in his ears?"

"Well, a parent's lot in life and death is disappointment." Hentzau gave me a flashing, careless smile, and I recalled that he had driven his own mother to her grave with a broken heart. "But I doubt that was Michael's concern. He is a cautious man, our duke. He spends too long in darkness."

"We all do that."

"You may. I don't fear the day." He was crossing the drawbridge as he said that. It was early afternoon, and the sun slanted across the moat, washing the sodden black stone with light, spilling gold over him like the spendings of some Greek deity. He turned to look at me, his dark hair haloed like a saint, smile bright as the sun, and a line from some play or poem came to my thoughts unbidden. *Cover her face; mine eyes dazzle; she died young.*

He was beautiful, and I was angry, and it had been a great deal too long. Hentzau cocked his head at me. I told him, "Inside."

We went to one of the Tower rooms, sparsely furnished with ancient pieces. Hentzau shut the door but didn't bolt it. He seated himself in a large carved wooden chair, arranging his somewhat dishevelled and travel-stained clothing with all the air of a lord in silks and velvet, and extended one lithe leg. "So, my Detchard. Are you going to help me with my riding boots?"

There were devils dancing in his eyes, and I was so tired of this absurd country and its thrice-damned duke. I had no desire to play lackey indefinitely to a sulking nobleman in the mountains; I had watched Michael strike my friend a coward's blow and done nothing about it. The next thing, I thought with disgust, would be that Michael would strike me and I would allow it.

"I am growing soft," I said aloud.

"I'm not," Hentzau said, giving himself a stroke to indicate as much. "Are you going to come here, or do you think of nothing but what pleases Michael?"

I came over. I knelt. I took hold of his boot—black leather, its usual gleam dulled by dust—and stroked its smooth surface, then up, up Hentzau's calf, sliding my hand over his leg, feeling the swell of muscle. Up further, with both hands now, running my thumbs down the insides of his taut, parted thighs. Hentzau was breathing hard, eyelids lowered, lashes dark and delicate.

"I'm not taking off your damned boots," I told him, words hoarse and harsh in my throat.

"I don't mind leaving them on."

I could see as much. His prick pushed against the tight cloth of his breeches, so that it would be a matter of charity, if not medical urgency, to release it. I stroked the bulge instead, running my fingers over its outlines until he moaned. It was good to see the mocking smile wiped off that handsome face for once.

I reached for the buttons at his waist. He inhaled, a tiny gulping gasp that I doubt he intended, shifting to give me access, and I pulled and pushed cloth aside to let his stiff prick spring free.

He was watching me under those drooping lids, with need and satisfaction too, much as if he imagined he had the whip hand of me now. That was his youth showing, the peculiar conviction that a hard prick is a source of power rather than a vulnerability, not to say a weakness.

As weaknesses go, his was delightful, slender and not too long for my purposes, the skin soft as I wrapped my fingers around it and slid them up and down. I leaned forwards, closer, so my lips hovered above and he could feel my breath, wrapping my fist around the root of his prick and pushing back when he attempted to thrust towards me. He gave a frustrated snarl. "Get on, damn you."

"Patience, boy."

"I don't have to be patient."

"Oh, but you do."

Because after all, what could he do seated in a chair, impeded by his riding breeches pushed around his hips, with I the larger and stronger? I saw the realisation dawn on him as I stroked and caressed him, slid a hand between his legs to his tight balls, skimmed his prick with my lips, until he gave a laughing, frustrated cry and squirmed under my hands. "Christ damn you, Detchard!"

"Well?"

"I implore you," he said. "By your kind grace, my worthy companion in arms, by the bond of chivalry and service in which we ride, suck my God-damned prick."

"Better," I said, and took him into my mouth.

And oh, the pleasure of that. I watched his fingers flex on the arms of the chair, and then his hands moved to my head. I had no long locks to which he might cling—I kept my hair short, and Nature was depriving me of what there was at a tiresome rate—but his fingertips closed on my scalp, betraying his need in a delightfully satisfactory manner. He was hot and hard and smooth against my lips, hips jerking, and I pushed forwards and took him all the way down.

Hentzau groaned pleasingly, and I went to work, sliding the circle of my lips up and down his shaft, working my hands under him to cup his balls. He shifted, pliant in his pleasure, and I slid one finger a little further, a teasing nudge between taut buttocks, and felt him twitch away, just a fraction.

Interesting. I made a mental note that my cocky young devil might not be so steeped in sin that I could not debauch him further, and let my hand rest, neither advancing nor retreating, while I pulled back to lavish the plump head of his prick with my tongue. Pressing, caressing, licking, and touching, slowing when I tasted the tang that told me he was close to spending. I was hard as a spear myself after those damned months of waiting, cock uncomfortably constricted, the pressure alone bringing me close myself, along with the pleasure of Hentzau's temporary enslavement.

To hell with it. I fumbled at my own buttons one-handed, got myself out, and fucked my own fist with a tight grip. Next time, I thought, I would turn him over and take that tense arse for my own pleasure, and that thought nearly did it for me, such that I gave up finesse and sucked him like a Paris whore, hard and fast, hollowing my cheeks with the effort. He grabbed at my hair with an urgent obscenity, his breath sped and hitched, and he came, spilling into my throat, with a breathy series of gasps for all the world as if he laughed. He would make more noise than that bent over a bed, I thought, and my imaginings tipped me over the brink so that I spent on the stone floor in spasms, his prick still deep in my throat, his spunk bittersweet in my mouth.

And then he was done, and we were trapped together in that endless moment, those terrible few seconds after climax when muscles relax and one becomes aware of the discomfort, stupidity, or indignity of one's position. I knelt still, hands and mouth holding him; he sat sprawled and half-naked.

I will admit to a moment's concern. I was punched in the head once at this point, a cur's blow by a man who took the pleasure but resented whatever he felt it did to his masculinity. I gave him the thrashing he deserved, including a few well-directed kicks that should have put him off any activity with anyone for some time to come, but still the memory came to mind and made me wary.

I let Hentzau's softening prick drop from my mouth, waiting. He opened those endlessly dark, long-lashed eyes and looked into mine, and that glorious smile dawned.

"Great God, Detchard. Why Michael hired you merely to cut throats, I cannot imagine. The man has no imagination."

"I've not even cut a throat for him yet," I pointed out, sitting back.

"No indeed. Your skills have been quite wasted until now."

"That was time well spent," I agreed, and found myself smiling. I am not a sentimental man, as is doubtless clear. I have always liked a lusty, laughing, careless partner who did not wish for mawkishness or impossibilities, a fellow with whom one might drink, fight, or fuck, and by God I had one here. "And now?"

He blew out his cheeks with comical exhaustion. "You'll have to give me a moment."

I couldn't help but laugh. "I need significantly more than a moment, you bloody spring-pricked boy. I meant the duke. What do you know of his intentions? Is he to remain here sulking like Achilles in his tent?"

"I couldn't say. I know only that he has fallen at the first hurdle. If he does not get up, this will be a sorry service."

"Will you remain?" I asked. If the rats intended to leave Michael's sinking ship, I might have a better chance to achieve my aim here.

"Mph. I was minded to consign him to the devil when he struck me. But I suspect his anger now is because he has realised his mistake. I have a feeling he may still act, and we shall see some fun if so."

"By fun, you mean the overthrow of the anointed king?" I enquired.

"He's not anointed, and that is the nub of it. The coronation is set for a month hence, and he is not the true king until that day. At the moment Rudolf the Red does not reign, dear Detchard: he merely rules. He has the title by courtesy and his father's blessing, but it may not be too late yet for a determined man with more friends than morals to make a play for all. *That* is what I call fun."

"I dare say it is," I remarked, sitting back on my heels. "It is certainly more my idea of fun than kicking my feet in this draughty dungeon."

"And I dare say you and I might keep each other entertained while we wait, and be damned to the duke's edicts." He nudged at my thigh with one booted foot, rubbing the leather against cloth.

"I have nothing better to do, I suppose," I said. "Why not?"

On such decisions do the fate of men and kingdoms turn. I told you hard pricks are dangerous.

CHAPTER SEVEN

Michael was not seen for three days. He had his meals sent to him in solitude for the first two, then he called for Antoinette. There was a bruise on her face still; she made no effort to cover it with powder and walked with her back straight. She did not speak to me beyond conventional politenesses, and when Michael summoned her to his room, she went.

We did not have much leisure for talk anyway. Michael sent orders for the Ruritanians of the Six to go to Strelsau and gauge public feeling; de Gautet and I made ourselves seen in Zenda and the other large towns, acting as a wet blanket on a couple of rowdy gatherings celebrating Red Rudolf's accession, though not by force. If we were to upturn the succession for Michael, and in truth I doubted it was possible now, he'd need the appearance of law on his side.

Bersonin did not come out with us, and soon enough we found out why.

Michael had emerged from his sulky seclusion while we rode on his orders, and now summoned us all back. We gathered in the Tower around the table one evening. It was bright summer but very little light ever made its way through those thick stone walls, and we were men of shadows as we gathered: Hentzau, Lauengram, and Krafstein; de Gautet, myself, and Bersonin, who sat at Michael's right hand and looked intolerably smug.

"Gentlemen," Michael said. "You all know how we stand. My father thought me to be the better man for Ruritania, just as the people do, yet he was old and cowardly and dared not defy tradition. Rudolf is to be king, though he is a drunken swine, a man with no love for his native soil, a despoiler of women, a gambler, a coward where he cannot be a bully. We all know that. The people know that. Krafstein, speak of your work."

Krafstein coughed modestly. "Sadly, the new king's glory in his own position has outweighed any restraint, or judgement. He has celebrated immoderately, and the word of those private indulgences has been spread through Strelsau and beyond. Some intimate tales from his past have found their way to the republican news-sheet"—he directed a small bow to Hentzau, who waved his hand modestly—"and the people murmur at what sort of king this pleasure-loving, self-indulgent sot may be. There is concern in the streets of Strelsau."

"And in the great houses too," added Lauengram. "People accept that Rudolf will be king, but in private at least they do not anticipate it with confidence. It is feared what he will do without his father to rule him. He made an attempt at seduction on the Lady Helga von Strofzin, you know, the day after the king's death, as a celebration of his accession."

"The art of seduction is to get the other party's consent against their better judgement," Hentzau observed. "In this case, Princess Flavia came running to stop him when she heard the screaming."

"I shall bow to your expertise as to what constitutes seduction," Lauengram said. "Flavia was enraged, and so was the Graf Strofzin, but the king is the king."

"Not until he's crowned," Michael said, with meaning in his tone. He looked around at us, face by face, taking each one of us in. "My fool brother has made himself an object of fear, anger, and disgust. The country is stirring, low and high. If he caps it all with an act that shows his contempt for not just those he meets, but the whole kingdom, the crown and Church together—the people will rise."

"What act?" I asked.

Michael smiled. "What would you say of a king too drunk to attend his own coronation?"

"Given the amount Rudolf puts away, he'd have to drown himself in a wine barrel to achieve that end," Hentzau said.

"No need for that," Michael said. "Bersonin?"

"A little powder," said the Belgian softly. He had thin lips, the livid kind, and kept them over his browned teeth when he spoke, so his mouth sometimes seemed merely a bloodless cut in his face. "A bottle of wine, of noble vintage, a gift to the king, with just a little powder mixed in. I can introduce it with the slimmest needle; the cork closes up around the piercing to make the tampering almost undetectable."

"And what does the powder do?" I asked.

"Simulates the effect of drunkenness—oh, so well. We know Rudolf will carouse the night before his crowning. But the next morning a splash of cold water will do no good. He will reel and stagger; he will shout and be quarrelsome. He may be lecherous. Perhaps he may vomit in the cathedral. Who knows?"

"Bersonin has demonstrated the powder to me, on two servants," Michael said. "The effect is quite remarkable."

"And would not be suspected, I suppose," Lauengram said slowly. "The way the man has behaved recently . . ."

"He turns up drunk in the cathedral, in front of the entire populace," Hentzau said, sounding awed. "My God. Now I imagine him getting confused by the ceremonial robes and attempting to ravish the cardinal."

Michael barked with laughter. I said, "What if his men realise he can't be sobered up and postpone the coronation, claiming illness?"

"On the morning, with the city full of people waiting? There can be no excuse."

"And we all know his excuses," Lauengram added. "He has been 'ill' too often."

"If he arrives drunk, it will be a disaster," Hentzau said. "If he does not, with the people waiting and the flags flapping in the breeze, it will be a riot. Curse it, Bersonin, it's brilliant."

I thought he would have been wiser to congratulate Michael; our duke's expression suggested so. He only said, "There is much to be done. We must keep feeling running high in Strelsau. And I must be positioned to seize the moment. I have been—as you all saw—publicly loyal to my brother. Nobody can accuse me of attempting to sway the Senate or people on the night my father died. We must continue with this course so the Red loyalists believe me beaten."

"You presented that appearance on the night of the succession admirably," Hentzau said. "I suppose you have been playing the game to this end all along. I salute your remarkable foresight."

"I salute Ruritania's lord-in-waiting," I said, and I pushed back my chair and led the others in a toast to Duke Michael, and his plan to ruin his brother's life.

"I suppose you had to say that," I remarked to Hentzau later.

"He hit me in the face."

"Still."

Michael had retired to his apartments after giving us our orders. Lauengram, Hentzau, and Krafstein would be leaving for Strelsau on the morrow, to keep us fully informed of the king's movements. De Gautet, as a Frenchman, had been charged with finding the most irresistible and rare bottles for Bersonin to doctor. I was to be Michael's close guard as he toured his lands and displayed his good rule, since he feared that his brother, now unchecked by their father, might have ill intent towards him. Accordingly, the party had broken up. Hentzau had brought a flask of wine up to my room and seated himself in the chair as I threw a few clothes into a travelling bag.

"What do you think of the scheme?" I asked. "Will it succeed?"

"If they can pull off the poison, there's every chance," Hentzau said thoughtfully. "There's the rub, of course. Bersonin has no way to know if the king will drink a single glass or half the bottle. How is he to calculate the dose? If Rudolf takes too much and dies—ugh. Or suppose he splits the bottle with a companion, and the ruse is discovered that way. This is high treason we're engaged in, you know. Ruritania still uses the axe for that here, though it's been a few years since it was required."

"Afraid?"

"Oh, pshaw, merely considering the possibilities. It's damned daring and I don't think Michael will have a better chance to unseat Rudolf."

"But if he unseats him, will Michael have the throne?" I asked. "What happens if the Senate and people conclude that Flavia is red, and thus right?"

"It's unlikely. That might happen if Rudolf dies of his disgrace and Michael can be squarely and openly blamed for it, but I wouldn't like to put a wager on her odds. No, I think this is Michael's best hope. I'm merely kicking myself that I took his part openly. If I were still of Rudolf's company, I could have ensured he drank exactly what was required."

"Why did you change sides?" I asked. "I heard you were the king's drinking companion."

"For a while." Hentzau tossed back a mouthful of wine. "He was a bore."

"Whereas Michael's charm is irresistible," I responded, perhaps unwisely. It was easy to forget that Hentzau and I were not companions, not on the same side.

Hentzau gave that boyish, unrestrained laugh of his. "Quite. No, I merely felt life might be more interesting on this side of things. I was, I think, probably right. Are you going to pack all evening?"

"Have you better ideas?"

We stripped naked this time, Hentzau in his usual careless way, tossing clothes over my floor. He didn't make any effort to build anticipation; perhaps he didn't need to. He was as trim and taut unclothed as one might hope, finely muscled without bulk, well proportioned, with a youthful look that belied his experience and doubtless devastated men and women across Ruritania. I have never been a fool for youth, but Rupert Hentzau in his prime was a thing of joy, laughing and confident, angel-faced and devil-eyed, and I found myself hoping he would not cause any angry Elphberg to order his death, whether for treason or insolence.

I undressed more slowly. I knew I looked well, for those who did not demand smooth youth; I was marked by scars and Indian sun, and Hentzau's eyes were searching and appreciative as I took my time—coat, waistcoat, shirt, displaying myself to advantage. I should, I thought, teach him the virtues of patience and control. He would need them one day, if he lived long enough to age.

I sat on my bed and extended a booted foot to him. He laughed, almost incredulously. "Please. Take off your own damned boots. And get on."

"Your problem is, you have a handsome face," I told him. "If you didn't, you'd have to learn to be a damned sight better at this."

"I *beg* your pardon?"

"Hentzau, Hentzau. If I had taken your boots off for you earlier, I could have had you writhing on the floor and begging me to do what I wished with you before I was halfway done with your prick."

He opened his mouth, briefly silenced, and came back with, "Then why didn't you?"

"Because I have patience, and finesse. Which you also lack."

"I've had no complaints," he said indignantly.

"I dare say you're finished before anyone has time to voice them."

He choked. I went on before he could articulate what would doubtless be a strong rebuttal. "I like youthful confidence. We can fuck as you choose, pretty Rupert; you can take what you want and I'll gladly oblige you. But sooner or later, I will teach you to give, and you'll thank me."

"I prefer the part where you oblige me, old man." Hentzau looked affronted, and aroused, and decidedly curious, and I wondered when the little fool might see the danger of his own arrogance. Bed was a safer place for that lesson than a duke's table, and certainly better than a swordfight.

Not that it was my job to save his neck, but he was lovely, and it would be a shame to see him spoiled.

I let it go, pulling off my own boots and stripping bare without too much ceremony. I lay back, idly stroking myself, and he strode to the bed and sat over me, straddling my chest. His thighs were very strong, his prick mouthwatering.

"When you say oblige me . . ." he began.

"Anything you please."

As before, a flicker of uncertainty. I reached for him, grasping his prick in one hand, his firm arse in the other, and let my hands explore. Hentzau allowed that for a few moments then gave a grunt, thrusting into my hand indicatively.

"On your back," I suggested, and rolled him over to pleasure him with my mouth again. He groaned softly, then louder, thrusting into my throat, hands stroking my hair, and I worked him lightly but firmly for a few minutes before he tugged at my hair.

"Mmm?"

"A moment, a moment. I want . . ."

I lifted my head away. "What?"

Hentzau exhaled. "Can I be honest?"

"I doubt it, but carry on."

He grinned briefly. "How can I put this? I've more skills with women than men. By quite some way. I haven't done much more than handling, truth be told. You are in every way a more experienced swordsman than I."

I snorted. "I'm glad you admit it. What on earth did you do at school, if not fuck?"

"I didn't go to school. I had a tutor. And I have always preferred women to men, so I have always concentrated my energies there."

"But you're desperate now for the lack of quim?" I suggested.

"No, that's not it at all. Let's say my horizons have broadened with the years, but my experience has yet to catch up. Think of me as an explorer, a Columbus, gazing out over a New World."

"Preparatory to slaughtering all the natives?"

"Shh." He smiled, a rueful smile that mocked, for once, only himself. "Educate me, Jasper. I feel I have much to learn."

Oh, I educated him. I showed him how to suck a man, and put that clever mouth to good work; I took full liberty with his body, stroking and touching his skin, making him explore me in return till his fingers were confident and his mouth sure. I brought him to the edge of climax with hands and mouth till he whimpered for satisfaction, and told him he could have his completion only once he had brought me to mine, and the squirming eagerness with which he sucked me off showed that I had a bright pupil. I came in his mouth, and he coughed and swallowed and smiled at me, lips wet and shining, and I found myself wondering what it might be like to kiss them.

I did not do that. I turned face down and had him rub himself off against me, braced over me and sliding his prick along the crease of my arse, feeling the tickle of hair against my neck when he bowed his head, and cursed Michael again that he was sending us off in all directions the next day for the sake of a poxy tin crown.

Hentzau collapsed against me when he was spent, and I put an arm over him, rather than lie on it and numb the nerve.

"You're damned patient," he said once he had his breath back. "I begin to understand what you mean about waiting."

"I feel sorry for your women."

"There is no need, I assure you. It's only that— Well. I suppose I imagined men would want to do it differently, that's all. Faster. Less attentively."

"Thrust, grunt, spend?"

"Well. Yes."

"It has its place. But if one can take the time, why not?"

"True. You don't kiss," he observed.

"No."

"Or do you not kiss me?"

"I don't kiss."

"You know, that seems to me much of a piece with thrust, grunt, spend," he said thoughtfully. "Affections are for women, that sort of thing."

"I don't kiss because I don't care to," I said. "I fuck *attentively*, if that's the word you want to use, because I do care to. You can find plenty of men who like to kiss, and I have no doubt many women who'd prefer not to. Don't make assumptions; they get you killed."

"That seems a little harsh."

"I meant in a swordfight, but it probably applies to the bedroom too. I could tell you stories."

"I have no doubt. Do you fuck? I mean . . ." He made a gesture with his hands. I gave him a blank look. He repeated the gesture with extra movements, glowered at me, and said, "Buggery."

"Thank God, I thought you meant knitting. I do, yes. Either part."

"But not tonight?"

"When you want to fuck me, you can say so," I told him. "And when I want to fuck you, you'll know because I'll have made you want it so much you'll be pleading for it."

Hentzau laughed aloud, startled, but I rather thought intrigued. "And you call *me* arrogant."

"A swordsman should know his own skill."

"True enough. Ah God, was that the clock striking one?"

"I fear so."

"Hell's teeth. I must go to bed." He rolled away and sat up, stretching, then rose and began to gather up his scattered clothes, making them into a bundle under his arm.

"For God's sake, dress," I said as he headed for the door.

"Why? There are no women in the Tower."

"There are several men, and you and I are not supposed to be fucking."

"Oh, pshaw, what is that to anyone? Do you think de Gautet cares?"

"Michael cares."

"Be damned to him," Hentzau said. Out of bed, his usual arrogance seemed to be restored at once. "He can give commands when he's king."

"But—"

"This isn't England, Detchard. You won't be flogged or hanged or whatever they do for fucking in that damned rain-soaked moralising land of yours. It's not a crime here, neither of us has a reputation to lose, and Michael needs every man he can hold to him. Goodnight, sweet schoolmaster. It's been a pleasure."

On which he walked out, arse-naked, carrying his clothes under his arm and his boots by the heels so as not to mar their leather with thumbprints. I lay back on my bed and stared at the ceiling.

A moment later the door reopened and Hentzau stuck his head in. "*Are* you going to tell me what you were up to that night? I meant to seduce it out of you, but I forgot."

"Will you fuck off," I said, casting around for something sharp-edged and heavy to throw, and the sound of his laughter echoed down the corridor, unrestrained, as he walked away.

CHAPTER EIGHT

I f I were asked for advice on committing treason, the best I could suggest is that you get on with it. Those weeks of work and waiting, necessary as they were, seemed some of the longest of my life. I am not a nervous man and would find it a sad anticlimax to die of old age, but I could undeniably feel the headsman's axe poised above my neck as the messengers went back and forth.

In some ways Michael had the hardest task. Where his men were at work, he was at play, or at least play-acting. His role was to show himself as duke and to convey that he pledged his loyalty to the crown of Ruritania, no matter his feelings as to the man who wore it. He was gracious to the Red loyalists, and even lovingly rebuked those who shouted, "Michael for King." At least he had me thrash an insolent republican, which provided a break from the monotony. (I have no quarrel with democrats in principle, except that they are as much frauds and liars as the rest. It is often said that mankind will not be free till the last king is strangled with the guts of the last priest; if you ask me, the man who ordered the strangling would promptly step forth to proclaim himself Lord Protector, and it would all begin again.)

In public Michael was calm, gracious—one might almost say regal. In private he strode up and down and bit his nails; he thanked me for my cool head and then cursed me for my damned phlegmatic cold-blooded Englishness in the next breath. Letters flew back and forth. Hentzau galloped from Strelsau to Zenda with the most incriminating messages, and I have no doubt enjoyed himself hugely. Antoinette asked Michael if she could go to see the child to be out of his way; he cursed her roundly for wasting his time with domestic trivia, and slapped her face to boot.

"God, I want him dead," she said in a rare moment that we could walk together. "*God*, I hate him."

"If you told Rudolf's party of the plans afoot here, you could see him beheaded," I pointed out.

"And you too, probably. But that wouldn't get me Lisl back. He has told me I will only see her again if I obey him; I have no idea where in the world she is. I don't know what to *do*. I should have had you hunt for her from outside. Except he had me watched in Paris, he says; maybe a watcher would have been seen. I'm coming to believe he watches me all the time. It's what he wants me to think, but—"

"Stop," I said, not liking the way her voice was rising. "Wait. If he pulls this coup off, he'll have no leisure for foolery, and I imagine he'll want you gone. If he fails, I'll see about persuading the others to flee, and then I'll take the bastard apart."

So we waited, and worked, and then quite suddenly we heard that Rudolf had demanded the day of his coronation be brought forwards, causing vast inconvenience to his subjects, whose preparations all had to be completed in a rush. He was ripely cursed around the country for this, but it made no odds in the Tower; our preparations were well in hand. Michael fretted that his brother suspected a plot. For myself, I was simply relieved that it was time.

We had learned that the king was determined on a carouse before his coronation, but that his keepers had succeeded in persuading him against his preferred haunts of brothels and drinking dens. He was to go hunting, and he was to do it in the forests outside Zenda. This was a favoured location of his on the few occasions he hunted, supposedly because it was the most convenient chase to Strelsau, in fact because it irritated his brother. He would be attended only by his manservant and his regular nursemaids: the stern Colonel Sapt, a loyalist of the late king, and the more personable Fritz von Tarlenheim, who caroused freely and posed as Rudolf's friend.

"They will be at the hunting lodge, all three, no other companions," Michael said. "The bottle has been sent."

"So near to Zenda, though." Krafstein's nerves were showing. "It is cursed ill luck. If something goes wrong, with him so close by—"

"If something goes wrong the duke will be blamed, were the king next door or at the other end of the country," Lauengram pointed out.

"It will not go wrong," Bersonin said. He was entirely calm, demonstrating what I can only describe as post-coital satisfaction at having poisoned his bottle. I have rarely met a man who so loved his work. "I have judged the dose carefully. One glass alone will have a strong effect, and more will not kill him. He can drink half the bottle if he chooses. It will succeed."

The king was to spend the night at a hunting lodge, a rude little place run by the mother of one Johann, Michael's gamekeeper. He would sleep there; in the morning Sapt and von Tarlenheim would come to Zenda to meet Ruritania's Second Regiment, known as the Duke's Light Cavalry, who would provide the king with a guard of honour to take him to the station. Michael had begged that distinction for his regiment in the most courteous terms, to show, he said, that his sword and his men were at the king's service; it was led by a noble major of unquestioned loyalty to the crown. The party would ride to the station at eight o'clock to meet the special train; the king would be in his palace at Strelsau by ten, and the parading started at noon.

If we succeeded, the king would be disgraced and displaced and Michael would rule. If we failed, Red Rudolf would be crowned God's anointed, and if we utterly buggered it, we would probably be dead by the end of the week. It made life interesting, I suppose.

We were all on edge the night before. Michael had gone to Strelsau to await his brother and get himself well out of the way, leaving Antoinette behind. He believed he might be able to form an alliance with Flavia even now. She disliked him but she despised Rudolf, the more since his attempt on her lady-in-waiting, and she would no longer be permitted to refuse his hand. She might well accept Michael as the lesser of two evils if she saw a chance to be rid of her kingly cousin.

Michael took only Lauengram and Krafstein with him. We foreigners would give the wrong impression for a man who wanted to present himself as Ruritania's true son, and Hentzau's reputation as a carouser with the king was not something with which the duke wished to be associated.

So we waited. I walked a while with Antoinette. She went to bed early; the four of us played a few desultory hands of cards and retired rather than sit in one another's company.

Hentzau came to my room. I did not so much as let him disrobe, but sucked him off as he stood till he staggered and gasped. We heard footsteps in the hall, pausing outside the door, which I assumed to be the creeping thing Bersonin; Hentzau only laughed, and begged to return the favour in the coarsest terms. It passed the time.

And then it was morning. We were all up by six. We dressed as a duke's gentlemen should and rode down to Zenda town, where the regiment was lined up in rows in the square, in its truly ridiculous dress uniform, trappings and medals shining in the sun, horses stamping. The people watched admiringly, and went about in their own best clothes, for it was a national holiday. Bunting flapped in the breeze, some of it in the king's colours, much of it in the duke's. There were baskets of flowers everywhere, and it was a bright, sunny day that was bidding fair to be hot.

"It's quarter to eight," Hentzau said from his position next to me. "How is it that the king's men are not here?"

He said that loudly, very much for the benefit of those around us. I replied in kind, remarking, "Perhaps they slept late," and heard sardonic laughter from our listeners, all of whom knew what it meant when the king slept late.

I should have liked to talk to him properly, for all the good speculation would do. We did not know how Sapt and von Tarlenheim might proceed with an obviously intoxicated king on their hands, whether they would seek help in Zenda or attempt to get him to the railway station and into Strelsau unobserved. At least they had not turned up as though all were well, or indeed to wail that the king was dead.

Eight o'clock struck, and the people waited. The half hour chimed, and they waited still. By nine the horses were restive, the sun was promising discomfort, and the mutterings were loud. *They aren't coming. No message sent. Insult. Dishonour. Disgrace.*

"This is a damned discourteous way for a king to treat his soldiers," Hentzau said to the square in general, and there was a stirring of applause.

We left the square at half past nine, with a mass of angry, insulted citizens behind us murmuring against their feckless king, and rode a little way out of town where we could speak.

"Well, it looks like the bottle worked," de Gautet said. "I congratulate you, Bersonin."

"We cannot yet be sure. They may simply have gone straight to Strelsau," I observed. "Perhaps they did not trust Michael's honour guard."

"That would be a damn fool way to start a reign, by insulting the army," Hentzau said. "What do you say, gentlemen? Shall we go and see?"

"Is that wise?" de Gautet asked.

"It's natural enough," I said. "We know where the king lay last night; we are concerned that his men did not arrive this morning. We go to discover if we can be of aid to His Majesty or His Majesty's men, should some unforeseen disaster have occurred."

"That's good enough for me," Hentzau said with a grin, and clapped his heels to his horse.

It was not much of a lodge. I dare say I am too used to British imperial magnificence, or the riches of Indian princes; Ruritania's trappings are decidedly less grand. This was a one-storey wooden bungalow, and it appeared deserted.

"Hi, the house!" Hentzau called, dismounting with his usual grace. "Hello?"

"The old woman should be here, at least," de Gautet said with a frown. "Johann's mother, what's her name. Hello, Frau Holf?"

There was still no answer. The lodge door was shut, but in the way of the countryside, not locked. I turned the handle and went in.

The room thus revealed was a scene of debauchery. The table seemed to have been untouched since the previous night: it held a litter of dishes with the congealing remnants of a large meal, and four place settings, well used. The candles were burned to their sockets, and a truly startling number of empty bottles lay scattered around. A dusty wicker-covered flagon was among them, and Bersonin's loving smile told me that this was the fatal bottle.

"It seems the king dined well," he said.

"It seems nobody cleared up after him," I added. "Where is the housekeeper?"

"Never mind that," Hentzau said. "It was the king, von Tarlenheim, and Sapt here, is that not right?"

"That was the plan," de Gautet agreed.

"So who the devil used the fourth knife and fork?"

As Hentzau spoke, I heard another sound, a faint noise as of a muffled cry. It came from a far door. I threw it open, drawing my sword, and revealed stone stairs going downward. The noise came again, and a grunt, and I ran down the stairs to see a cellar. There was a torch burning on the wall, two bodies lying on the floor, and a wide-eyed little serving-man staring at me.

"The duke's murderers!" he bleated. "Help! Murder! Poison! Help!"

"Shut up," I told him, and put my sword to his throat.

The others had been close behind me. Hentzau strode past to one of the recumbent bodies, crouched to see in the dim torchlight, and rapped out, "Detchard! Look here!"

I lowered my blade, nudging the servant over to Bersonin's charge, and turned to see what Hentzau had found. And stood, and stared, because of all the damned unexpected things I have ever seen in my life, this was without doubt the damnedest.

The slumped man on the floor was the King of Ruritania.

"Good God almighty," I said. "They just left him here?"

"It's the king!" de Gautet said, catching up.

"What the hell. Is he dead?"

"Breathing, but out like a light," Hentzau said. "He's drenched; they must have been throwing water on him. He doesn't look like he'll wake soon, if ever. Well done, Bersonin. You put him into a coma, you stupid bastard."

"No." Bersonin knelt by the king, glared at him, slapped the slack face. "No! The cursed sot must have drunk the entire bottle. Damn him, damn him!"

"Where are his men?" de Gautet demanded. "Gone for a doctor?"

"You," I said to the serving-man. "Talk. What happened? Where are Sapt and Tarlenheim?"

He spat at me. He had nerve, I'll give him that.

There were urgent noises coming from the floor—from, I realised, the other body, which proved to be that of an old woman, tied up in the most peculiar way with silk handkerchiefs, including one stuffed in her mouth. Hentzau sliced away her bonds and helped her to a seated position, waving irritably when de Gautet began to question her. "For heaven's sake, get the lady a drink first. Please, Mother, don't distress yourself. What villain did this outrage to you?"

Rupert of Hentzau, solicitous protector of old age. It was enough to make a cat laugh.

We were in a wine cellar. De Gautet plucked a bottle from the shelves and Hentzau gave her drink, arm around her shoulders. "There, that's better. You are Frau Holf, yes? Can you tell us what happened?"

"It was the king's men," the old lady said. "Drunks and villains, all of them. They found me listening to their talk this morning, as my sons asked me to do for the duke, and they hit me and tied me up, the cowardly swine. Afraid of an old woman."

She sneered at the serving-man. He spat a vile epithet at her. I backhanded him across the face and requested she continue.

"Last night the king drank like the sot he is, and this morning he could not be awoken. They—Sapt, von Tarlenheim—conceived an imposture. They decided to present a fraud to the Almighty and the people."

"A what?" I said.

"A fraud! A man who can impersonate the king!"

"That's *quite* unlikely to work," Hentzau said, with some understatement. "Rudolf has not been greatly in the country, but I still think people might notice."

"No, sir, no," Frau Holf said urgently. "He is as like to the king as two peas in a pod. They shaved his moustache off—I saw his face, and he is the very image. With my own eyes, I saw it. And he has gone to be crowned in Strelsau in the king's place!"

"She's mad," Bersonin said.

"I don't think so." I had been watching the servant's expression, the triumph under the fear. "You there, is it true? Do they have an impostor?"

"Go to hell. I tell you nothing, poisoners."

"Who is this man?" demanded de Gautet. "The fourth diner, upstairs, was that him? Where the devil did he spring from?"

"They met him in the forest by chance," the old woman said. "An Englishman, some bastard of the old king's or a bastard's son. I don't know. The king called him cousin and jested of their resemblance."

"A bastard, or a throwback," Hentzau said. "A man with a look of the king, coming here to see his royal relative crowned, I suppose. Of course Rudolf would invite a doppelgänger to dinner. He loves his own face dearly."

"He dined here," I said slowly. "Slept here. They all woke to find the king in this state. And Rudolf wouldn't wake up. Sapt and Tarlenheim will have been panicking, wondering if a dead-drunk king today would be a dead king by evening—"

"And then realised they had a double to hand," Hentzau finished. His eyes held a look of unholy awe. "It's magnificent. I take off my hat to them."

"You stupid, poncing prick!" Bersonin snarled. "They'll kill us all!"

"You deserve it," the manservant said. "Murderers, villains, betraying your king, the true son, for your bastard duke—"

"Shut him up," I told Bersonin, and turned back to Hentzau. "We need to think about this. I—"

The old woman gave a hoarse shriek, clapping her hands to her mouth, eyes widening. I swung round once more to see Bersonin let the serving-man's body fall. His throat gaped, wide and red.

"Oh, for Christ's sake!" I said, with I think pardonable annoyance. "What the devil did you do that for?"

"Silence," he said. "Now and later. We can have no witnesses."

The old woman shrank back fearfully. Hentzau patted her arm soothingly. "Please, don't be afraid. You have no need to worry; the duke protects his own."

"This is not a fit business for a woman," I said, somewhat too late. "De Gautet, will you take this lady outside for some fresh air?" I waited till I heard footsteps and the outer door close. "Well, gentlemen, what now? We must assume Sapt and Tarlenheim will be back soon—"

"No, we must not," Hentzau said. His eyes were bright. "If an impostor is being crowned in Strelsau, they will be flanking him every moment of the day. It's their necks if anyone learns they've presented a fraud to the people, or the princess, or God. There would be rioting; they'd be lucky to live until the executioner got to them. They *have* to keep with the play-actor to make it work. That's why the king is left here like lumber, under that fool's guard."

"They couldn't send anyone to collect him," I agreed slowly. "Far too dangerous. They had to leave him here. And they'll come back to get him once the festivities are done—hoping, I suppose, that he will have slept it off and can take his rightful place with nobody noticing."

"They must be mad," Bersonin said.

I shrugged. "People see what they expect. If it's a sufficient resemblance, if you did not know the king had a doppelgänger, if you expected to see Rudolf…"

"Detchard is right. People are idiots," Hentzau said. "Although Flavia is not. Well, this *will* be interesting."

"You may say so," I said. "Right, there is no point avoiding the question. What the buggery are we to do with the king?"

Bersonin's thin lipless smile widened. He took a step forwards, knife in hand, and came up short with my blade against his belly.

"Restrain yourself," I said. "We're still discussing this. There are two decisions to make. Whether we take him with us or leave him here, and whether we do it with him alive, or dead."

"To leave him here alive is to resign the game, and we'd need to start running now," Hentzau said. "If we kill him, Colonel Sapt still has a crowned king in Strelsau. And Sapt dearly loathes Duke Michael."

"You think he'd put an impostor on the throne for good?" I asked.

"I don't know. But we can hardly object that their man isn't the real king if our only proof is that we killed the true Rudolf ourselves. Whereas if we take him…" Those demons danced in Hentzau's eyes. "Sapt can have his false king on the throne; we'll have a real ace in our pocket."

"One who could tell tales of imprisonment in Zenda."

"True. But Zenda has a deep moat that will hide a body, if it comes to that."

"And in any case, we can't leave him here," I said. "If I were Sapt and found him dead I'd get rid of the impostor, set up a new murder scene, and accuse Michael." And I had a good idea of Michael's likely response, in that uncomfortable circumstance. He would cast the blame on his hired bravos and watch us all go to the block without remorse. "There's no choice. We'll take him with us, alive, and kill him if we must." I sheathed my blade, and Hentzau and I heaved the unconscious body up the stairs. It never ceases to amaze me how heavy these are.

De Gautet and the old woman were nowhere to be seen. We set Bersonin to keep watch, and had got the drugged king onto the back of one of the horses and covered in a cloak by the time the Frenchman returned, alone.

"What did you do with her?" I asked.

"Dealt with it. She had heard too much."

"Are you serious? You killed the old woman?" I said. "You— Oh Christ. Marvellous."

Bersonin sneered. "There can be no witnesses. You are weak."

"I'm surrounded by idiots," Hentzau said. "She was Max and Johann's mother, you bloody fool! How do you propose to explain that away back at the castle?"

"We'll tell them she's been packed off for safekeeping," I said. "De Gautet, we're borrowing your horse for the king. You and Bersonin clear up your mess. Properly, please, we don't want anyone finding her. You can ride back together."

"Maybe you can find someone else to murder on the way to keep your hands in," Hentzau added nastily. "Come on, Detchard. His Majesty's guard of honour can't wait."

CHAPTER NINE

We rode through the woods, Hentzau and I. We could not gallop, since we had to keep the horse that bore the unconscious king with us, and we had no rope to tie him to the beast's back. He may have fallen off once or twice.

I should have liked to gallop; the forest was full of noises, and I expected a hunter, woodcutter, passing peasant, or, since this was Ruritania, small child in a red-hooded cloak at any moment. We had our burden covered as best we could, but the fact was, never did two men commit high treason quite as obviously as we, riding off with a half-dead monarch on his coronation day, leaving two dead witnesses behind us. There comes a point at which a trail of corpses becomes a problem instead of a solution.

We didn't speak much. Hentzau said at one point, "Well, this is what you British call a lark," and laughed, for all the world as though we rode for pleasure.

We skirted the castle—even Hentzau would not ride up the great approach with our burden—and he went off to get a larger cloth to cover the king while I waited. Still breathing, no sign of waking. I had wondered what we would do if he regained consciousness and began to shout or struggle, and had been planning the most convenient route to the border accordingly; it was a relief when Hentzau returned with a bit of sacking. We carried him into the Tower, where I as the stronger lugged the fellow into one of the many rooms with stout doors and locks, and Hentzau took the horses off to the stable.

"Well," he said, once all that was done. "What now?"

"A message to Michael, I think. He must be concerned."

"Ah, the great British understatement." Hentzau checked the clock. "It's past noon. The player-king will be riding through the streets of Strelsau, cheered or booed. Or perhaps the imposture is discovered and the city is rioting as we speak."

"It must be a damned good likeness, or Sapt would not have dared attempt this."

"It must. Though Rudolf has been much out of the country, has never attended Senate meetings, and has been as far as possible avoided by Flavia's court," Hentzau said. "And mostly, well, if you thought a king looked slightly different on the day of his coronation, yet his closest companions seemed unaware of a change, would you conclude it was a different man, or simply chalk it up to lack of sleep?"

"We'll find out, I suppose. What message can we give Michael?"

"It must be carefully written, that's for sure." Hentzau gave it a moment's thought, then seized paper and pen and dashed off a note, which he showed me.

My lord duke

Regarding the jewel which you recently purchased via our Belgian friend: By some strange chance, it seems you have a counterfeit on your hands. I am delighted to say all's well and we have the original held safe at Zenda awaiting your pleasure.

Your humble servant

Rupert Hentzau

"All's well?" I repeated, with some incredulity.

"Well enough for me."

I decided not to argue; it would not be any use. "It will do; get it to him as fast as you may. I will close down the Tower. We want no servants here. Not a soul passes the drawbridge now but as commanded by Michael."

Hentzau nodded. "And one more task for us both, I think?"

"What's that?"

"Pack a bag. If this goes bad, we will both need to run as though the hounds of hell were at our heels."

"Teach your grandmother to suck eggs," I told him, in English. "I was running for my life when you were in the schoolroom cheeking your tutor." And he doubtless had no idea what that might entail, or the ways by which a man might slide out from the grasp of the avenging law. "Do you know the Schwanthalerhöhe district of Munich? There is an inn called the Hundsstüberl on Kazmairstrasse. A message left there will reach me eventually, should you find yourself in trouble."

"I have much to learn, I see." He flipped me a cheery salute and went to send the letter. I returned to the king.

Michael returned to the castle late that evening. He came to the Tower, with Krafstein and Lauengram at his heels, and a look of a man in the grip of a nerve-storm.

"What the devil has happened?" he barked. "What did your letter mean, *all's well*? How is it *well*, and who in seven hells was that man who took the crown?"

"Oh, it all went ahead, did it?" Hentzau asked with an air of intelligent interest, and I thought Michael would strike him.

I took over, giving a brief explanation of what we had found in the lodge and what we had done, including the two deaths. Michael listened, face tense. I could not tell if he thought we had done right or not. He heard me out, then said only, "And you have my brother here."

"Locked in. Still not awake."

"He must have drunk the entire bottle," Bersonin repeated for perhaps the seventh time.

Michael turned to him and de Gautet next to him. "What did you do with the servant's body? Detchard said only that you buried the old woman."

"We left him in the cellar where he fell," de Gautet said as if that were obvious. Hentzau made a quiet noise of despair, and I pinched the bridge of my nose. I had not even thought to ask such an obvious question as *did you hide both bodies?*

Michael exhaled through set teeth. "Fools. Fools to kill and fools not to conceal your kill. Go and send someone to hide the damned body. My manservant Max would be best, and remember he is brother to Johann, so *try* to ensure he doesn't find out you cut his mother's throat." He dismissed Bersonin and de Gautet with a gesture, and turned back to Hentzau and me. "And you pair. Did you reflect that you have committed me to open treason? Did it occur to you that you were kidnapping a *king*?"

"Very much so," I said. "But Colonel Sapt had outmanoeuvred us; our choice was to fight or to surrender utterly and leave him and Red Rudolf the field. We chose to fight."

"And it is not open treason yet," Hentzau said. "Nor can it be while Sapt presents the people with a false king. Was the ceremony completed?"

"And all the festivities. The play-actor was anointed by the cardinal, made vows to his people in the Lord's name, was cheered through the streets, and had his hand kissed by every dignitary in Strelsau." Michael's lips curved unpleasantly. "All of them grovelling to a fraud. When they learn what Sapt did—"

"He can't let them," Hentzau said. "If Sapt's man is revealed as a fraud, their lives won't be worth a penny more than—well, than ours. Sapt can't accuse you because he dare not say his man is not the king; you can't accuse Sapt without saying how you know his man is not the king. It's rather amusing, really."

"How good is the likeness?" I asked.

"Uncanny," Michael said, still glaring at Hentzau. "The man is like as two peas to Rudolf, if Rudolf were less dissipated. I think he must be Rudolf Rassendyll, brother to the English Lord Burlesdon. My great-grandfather or suchlike had an affair with the Countess of Burlesdon that ended in a duel, and left our mark on their family. I had heard one of their sprigs had Elphberg looks. But what devil of a coincidence brought him here?"

"More importantly, what will Sapt do now?" Hentzau asked. "He will have come back to exchange his pawns and collect the true king as soon as possible—which is to say, as soon as the play-actor could retire from his duties. He will find, or has already found, the lodge empty—"

"And if he gets there before Max does, he will see a murdered man on the floor," I added. "Which will doubtless be suggestive. But in any case, the lodge is near Zenda; he must assume we have snatched the king from his grasp."

"If he gets rid of the play-actor, he will have to raise a hue and cry for a king gone missing the day after his coronation," Michael said slowly. "The people will not be pleased. But will Sapt dare to keep an impostor on the throne?"

"We'll find out, I suppose," Hentzau said. "Shall you return to Strelsau?"

"With accompaniment," I said. "We are at war now, Your Grace, even if it is not open war."

"Do you think I do not realise that? I shall have you, de Gautet, and Bersonin with me. Hentzau, Krafstein, Lauengram, you stay to guard my brother here."

Lauengram and Krafstein had been notably silent through this; they both bowed now without enthusiasm. Doubtless they had already realised that there was no going back from here, but Michael's unsubtle means of thoroughly implicating his three Ruritanians in the treason did not escape them. Hentzau merely shrugged.

We thrashed the business out a little longer, without getting anywhere, and then Michael demanded to see his brother. Hentzau and I took him to the room where Rudolf lay, still out, but now snoring. Michael stared down at his brother, his monarch. He came to stand directly over him, then without warning delivered a punch, straight down, right into the unconscious man's belly.

"Sot," he said, and spat on his brother's face.

He turned and walked out. At the door he stopped. "This room is not secure. Put him in a cell and chain him. You and Krafstein will sleep in the Tower tonight, Hentzau. Be sure the drawbridge is raised."

He strode off down the corridor. We watched him go, then I turned to Hentzau with a raised brow. He shrugged. "Rudolf would do the same to him."

I didn't envy Ruritania its choice of masters, but I did not say so. I doubted Hentzau would care in the slightest, but the halls and corners of the Tower seemed very dark tonight, and the shadows full of listeners.

We moved the king down to one of the cells, chained him by one wrist, and locked the cell door. Hentzau stepped back with a sour look. "That's done. You are for Strelsau tomorrow, while I nursemaid the drunkard here. Shall we make the most of tonight?"

I nodded, and we headed up towards the habitable rooms together and stopped, because Krafstein was standing at the top of the stairs.

I gave him a nod. He stepped directly in front of me. "Excuse me, Detchard. I am requested to remind you of the duke's terms of your employment here."

"And now you have done so, yet you are still in my way."

His eyes flicked meaningfully to Hentzau. "And will remain so. Good night."

Hentzau leaned back, shoulders to the cold stone wall, with the appearance of a man settling down to watch the show. Krafstein did not shift. "The duke made certain stipulations as to your personal pleasures. You are expected to abide by those. He is informed that you have deliberately disobeyed his explicit order."

"Well, it would be awful to do that by accident," Hentzau put in cheerfully.

"Informed by whom?" I demanded. "As though I need ask. Bersonin, of course."

Krafstein shrugged. "He finds your ways distasteful."

"I should have more interest in his opinions if they were accompanied by competence. I would remind you, my friend, that I am not a debutante whose virtue has to be guarded."

"No. You are the duke's man, and he has given his orders."

"For Christ's sake," Hentzau said. "Morality doesn't suit you, Krafstein. Though it must be a nice change from finding schoolgirls for the so-particular Bersonin. I have not the strength for this absurdity; I'm going to bed. Bonsoir, mon cher Detchard. I trust you will find Strelsau amusing."

He strolled up towards Krafstein as he spoke. The pimp made way for him and gave me a smug smile. I contemplated wiping it off by means of kicking him down the flight of stone stairs, but made myself turn my back, and returned alone to the chateau, thoroughly irritated.

Considering the situation, and our shared guilt, one might have expected Michael to ingratiate himself to his men as best he could, but that was not our duke's way. He had insulted Bersonin and the proud de Gautet, made it clear to the three Ruritanians that they would be fully implicated in his treason, and chosen to dictate my pleasures. He was, in fact, telling us all that he held our lives in the palm of his hand, and we would be wise to bow our necks to the yoke.

Needless to say, I or any of the Six could have ridden for Strelsau and bought our pardon with an accusation against the duke. I didn't know if Michael wanted to assert his whip hand because he felt he had lost power to us, or to remind us that we were not made equal by our equal guilt, and in truth I didn't care. Michael considered us his to order and to use as much as ever, and I suspected that when this was over, if he came out on top, he would feel free to discard us in a permanent sort of way.

You may wonder why I stayed. Antoinette was my friend, and I owed her a debt, but she did not expect me to sacrifice my life for it. If I had been sensible, I dare say I should have fled, but I have never been one for wise decisions, and I was, in truth, intensely curious to see the game out. It is not every day one overthrows a monarch, after all.

We travelled back to Strelsau the next day. Michael had left Antoinette in his house there, apparently feeling secure in his power over her. I imagine it was scant consolation to him, for the burial party sent to the lodge had met resistance. Men, undoubtedly of the king's party, had been lying in ambush there when they arrived and had attacked, killing three of Michael's men in a savage melee. Our side had inflicted nothing but a slight bullet wound upon one of the assailants as he rode away. It was a bad defeat, and showed us that we had opposition on our hands.

Worse than that, Colonel Sapt had called Michael's bluff. Since he could not return the real king to the throne, he had left the impostor there. It was an extraordinary bit of daring, but evidently the fellow Rassendyll was throwing himself into the part, and playing the king with such charm and goodwill that I couldn't imagine why anyone actually believed him. Only the fact that he did not know the names of many important people made him seem like the real man.

It put Michael into a spitting rage. We all told him to stay calm—the deeper the imposture ran, the less possible it would be for Sapt to deny it if or when we revealed the sham. Michael did not agree.

"He is not just filling the place; he is fighting for the king he impersonates," he said bitterly. "Worse, he keeps up the pretence, as do I, so I must bow and scrape and kiss a charlatan's hand."

He insisted that we must come to get the measure of the man, and that was how I found myself in an anteroom in the Royal Palace at Strelsau, waiting to meet a forgery of a king.

It was absurd. We waited while the Duke of Strelsau paid homage to the King of Ruritania, and every man of us there knew the truth. I was grateful Hentzau was not present; I could all too easily imagine him saying something catastrophically accurate.

Michael entered arm in arm with the player-king, for all the world like loving brothers. Michael's expression was bland and smooth, but I could see the depth of rage in his eyes. He beckoned us forwards.

"These gentlemen are the loyalest and most devoted of Your Majesty's servants, and are my very faithful and attached friends," Michael announced with stately courtesy.

"On the last ground as much as the first, I am delighted to see them," replied the fraud.

We came one by one and kissed his hand—De Gautet, Bersonin, and then myself. The pale hand I took had one finger well bandaged up, and I wondered if the player-king had been one of those who ambushed and killed our men. I gave him an assessing look as I straightened from my bow. He returned it, I suspect because Englishmen warranted more of his time than foreigners, and said in English, but with a wildly overdone Ruritanian accent, "Ja, I am vell pleased to make your acvaintance."

What an outstanding prick, I thought, and had to bite my lip and bow again to hide my smile.

Nevertheless, I could not help but be impressed. The man was walking a tightrope blindfolded and enjoying every second of it; so much was clear. I recognised the look in his eyes, not unlike Hentzau's dancing demons. We could, I thought, expect fireworks.

I managed to find Antoinette alone that evening. Michael was obliged to go to one of many balls, and had not elected to bring her. Perhaps he did not wish to flaunt her in front of Flavia (who was rumoured to smile with new fondness upon her cousin the king); also, the ladies' fashion for bare arms did not sit well with bruises.

She was sitting in the garden, enjoying the cool night air, except that she did not seem to be enjoying anything. I came and sat by her. She didn't speak.

"Is it time to leave?" I said at last. "At least, to ask him for permission to go or beg him to let you stay out of the firing line? I'll stay and try to find Lisl. But I think you should go."

"Because his blows will only get harder and more frequent. Do you think I don't know how this works?"

"That, yes, but I meant you should go because if Michael loses this game, you will be damned by association. And if our heads are put on spikes together, nobody will look twice at mine."

She managed a smile at that. "Dear Jasper, your head will in any case be next to Rupert Hentzau's, so you don't stand a chance. Unless he betrays you all first to save himself, I suppose. *Do* you think Michael will lose?"

"Damned if I know. It's a stalemate for now."

"Michael says we can give the impostor a long rope to hang himself. That he will make a mistake and give himself away soon enough."

"Michael is wrong, to my mind," I said. "The impostor is a clever man, and a daring one. And a great deal more like a king than that crawling Red Rudolf. People want to believe in him."

"Particularly the Princess Flavia," Antoinette said. "They say she is growing fond of the king at last. This would be a cruel deception for her, if she comes to love the impostor."

"I'm starting to conclude that love is best avoided altogether," I said. "It is rarely anything but a bloody nuisance."

"I can't argue with that. You aren't in love with Hentzau, are you?"

"I?" I asked blankly. "Certainly not; I am not such a fool. That way madness lies, if ever I saw it."

"You're right there. He is far too fond of being loved. Far too fond of himself, even."

"I don't think that's fair," I said, with a perverse urge to defend him. "He's an arrogant sprat, but he is very young still. And he is amusing, he has conversation; he is a living man in that tower of gargoyles. I like him a great deal."

"And he is Michael's man. What if he stands in your way?"

I found I disliked that idea. "I hope it won't come to that. But none of it means I aspire to settling down in a cottage with roses around the door, with him or anyone."

She snapped her fingers. "Which reminds me. What happened to that fellow of yours, the serious one?"

"Henri? We parted. He is studying to become a priest, I hear."

She cackled. "You don't mean it. What a waste."

"I fear so. He said it was all or nothing, and since I couldn't give him anything like all, we settled for nothing."

"I'm sorry for it."

Henri was a good soul with an unfortunate taste for bad men, and he deserved happiness, but people rarely get what they deserve. He had wanted far more than I had to give, and I could not resent him for leaving me. "There was no other way. Rootless adventurers bound for a bad end have no right to dally with serious men. It wasn't fair of me."

"Love isn't fair," she said, with sudden harshness. "Love has brought me nothing but pain. I have loved twice, and both times it has bade fit to ruin my life. If I never love again, I shall be grateful."

"You deserve a man who adores you," I told her. "Find one, and we'll make sure he knows that if he lays a hand on you, I shall break his kneecaps with a hammer."

"Oh, Jasper, you are sweet. And I'll take you up on that if ever I can. Escort me in. I must pack; our master intends us to return to Zenda tomorrow."

CHAPTER TEN

Michael kept de Gautet, Bersonin, and me in Strelsau for the next few days. He was wise to do so. If I had been Colonel Sapt and had wanted the real king back, my first move would have been to kidnap Michael and extract the location from him. We kept by our master whenever he set foot in the streets, and became quite familiar with the faces of Sapt's watchers.

The other three of the Six remained in Zenda, guarding the prisoner. It was a marked change from how Michael had managed his men previously, and the player-king would have been a fool not to deduce that the king was there.

He didn't appear to care. Rassendyll was throwing himself into his pretence with glee, turning Red Rudolf's many deficiencies to account, charming his people with his newfound sober habits and desire to work, and squiring Princess Flavia with a charm that brought a blush to her pale cheek and a flutter to many a sympathetic heart. He was making Rudolf V a king, and there was damn all Michael could do about it.

"I want him gone," he snapped. "With him gone, we can act."

That was easier said than done. If the king were mysteriously murdered, all Ruritania would blame his brother, and as Rudolf's fitness for the throne grew, Michael's support was ebbing. He'd missed his chance once again, and knew it.

Not that I intended to point that out. "Have you orders for me, Your Grace?"

"Read this." Michael held out a letter. It was in a woman's handwriting.

If the King desires to know what it deeply concerns the King to know, let him do as this letter bids him. At the end of the New Avenue there stands a house in large grounds. The house has a portico, with a statue of a nymph on it. A wall encloses the garden; there is a gate in the wall at the back. At twelve o'clock tonight, if the King enters alone *by that gate, turns to the right, and walks twenty yards, he will find a summerhouse, approached by a flight of six steps. If he mounts and enters, he will find someone who will tell him what touches most dearly his life and his throne. This is written by a faithful friend. He must be alone. If he neglects the invitation his life will be in danger. Let him show this to no one, or he will ruin a woman who loves him: Michael does not pardon.*

"Is this meant to be from Flavia?" I asked, somewhat confused.

"Antoinette. She has been playing the wronged woman long enough; she can put that sorrowful face to use for me now."

I considered several responses, but settled for, "You dictated this to her?"

"Of course."

"And you think Rassendyll will believe it?"

"Turn it over."

I did. The same hand had written:

If you hesitate, consult Colonel Sapt. Ask him what woman would do most to prevent the duke from marrying his cousin, and therefore most to prevent him becoming king? And ask if her name begins with—A?

"A pleasing touch, I think," Michael said, with a smile of some self-congratulation.

"It is more convincing with that addendum. He will surely doubt that a woman with any self-respect would write such a thing at her lover's dictation." I mentally added another mark to Michael's tally. "Well, we shall see if it works."

"It will. He will come because a lady appeals—the man fancies himself a knight in a medieval land. He will doubtless expect attack and have men close by, of course."

"Indeed. Let us say he keeps his appointment: what would you have us do?"

"Assess the situation," Michael said. "Antoinette will paint a picture for him of the grave danger he is in, how he might be killed on the street at any moment. He is an earl's brother, not an adventurer; he will not wish to face death."

"He dealt with the gravediggers summarily enough."

"Anyone can kill from behind," said Michael, who ought to know. "If he understands that his life is forfeit, he may be inclined to fly. And if he is, let us grease his way. Offer him fifty thousand English pounds to leave. It is a better prize than a death in the shadows, or on the block if his impersonation is revealed."

"*Fifty thousand?*"

"It would tempt any man, and I want him tempted." His lips curled. "That would be the ideal outcome. I will wager that Sapt will be watching; it is quite possible he will kill his own man rather than see him change sides. And if *that* were to happen—"

"You could drop the true king in the moat, call Sapt a regicide, and seize the throne," I agreed. "It's certainly worth a try. And if he does not accept the offer?"

"Do what you can," Michael said. "If you have a chance to kidnap him privately and conveniently, or to kill him and remove the body, take it. If we can make the play-actor vanish, by whatever means, there will be a great hue and cry. We can plant word that the king has tired of virtue and fled to the fleshpots of Munich, betraying the princess and his people together, and in due course 'discover' him dying or dead of dissipation. We can fill him with opium to make sure."

"That is excellent," Bersonin said, probably because it involved poisoning.

"Marvellous," I said. "Then I shall speak to Mademoiselle de Mauban and make all ready for tonight."

She was seated in her bedchamber, looking out of the window. She was dressed for an evening party, complete with long satin gloves, in no way appropriate for the weather. I know nothing of women's fashion, but I knew Michael.

"He bruised your wrists, I suppose?"

"Only the left. He needed the right intact so I could write the letter."

"It was probably unwise not to agree at once."

"He's put me in the centre of his plot," she said. "My handwriting on a lure for the king. If this goes wrong, he's made sure I'll be on the block next to him. If I last so long, since he has also put me in a summerhouse with a man engaged in stealing a crown, whose life hangs by a thread."

"I'll be outside," I said for what that was worth. "Toni, I think you should vanish. I know you fear for your daughter, and Michael's spite, but if you aren't alive to look to her, I doubt anyone else will look to her either; Michael won't care when she is no longer a useful bargaining chip. You run, it's only sensible. I'll see if I can get him to send me to her, in the manner of Snow White and the huntsman, and if he won't do that, I'll just have to make him talk."

She shook her head. "I can't take the risk. I *can't*."

"You could look for her from outside. I'll help you."

"How? Michael has my bank books, my papers, everything. He has my jewels locked away each night. How can I search Europe with no money and a vengeful duke pursuing me? What will I do, return to earning on my back? I'm so tired of men. I've spent my life smiling and flattering and listening and soothing, pandering to their moods and raising their flaccid pricks, and I have had enough. I won't become some wandering magdalen howling for her lost child, and I will not leave while there is a chance to find Lisl." She kept her voice low, but it throbbed with passion. "I am going to do this, Jasper. I want my daughter and my money and some peace. And I will burn all Ruritania to ash if that's what it takes to get them."

Antoinette's appointment with Rassendyll was for midnight; accordingly Bersonin, de Gautet, and I arrived at the rendezvous at half past ten. The summerhouse was in the grounds of a grand but empty residence. The gardens were overgrown, the shrubbery excellent for concealment, if scratchy. Antoinette came directly from some soirée at just past eleven o'clock and went directly to the summerhouse. It was somewhat dilapidated with a rickety door that would not stand up to many kicks.

Rassendyll arrived at half past eleven, and the faint sound of hooves suggested he had a companion. He walked up the path alone, holding a bull's-eye lantern, and I was tempted to shoot him simply as punishment for making himself such an obvious target.

He let himself into the summerhouse, and I heard Antoinette, her marvellous voice pitched low and clear to carry well, even while she spoke as though agitated.

"Don't talk. We've no time. Listen! I know you, Mr. Rassendyll. I wrote that letter at the duke's orders."

"So I thought," Rassendyll said, as smugly as if he'd done something clever.

"In twenty minutes, three men will be here to kill you," she went on.

"Three—the three?"

"Yes. You must be gone by then. If not, tonight you'll be killed—"

"Or they will." He spoke with the kind of self-confidence that comes from never having faced serious opposition. I was taking quite a dislike to the player-king.

"Listen, listen!" Antoinette said, according to her script. "When you're killed, your body will be taken to a low quarter of the town. It will be found there. Michael will at once arrest all your friends—Colonel Sapt and Captain von Tarlenheim first—proclaim a state of siege in Strelsau, and send a messenger to Zenda. The other three will murder the king in the castle, and the duke will proclaim either himself or the princess—himself, if he is strong enough. Anyhow, he'll marry her, and become king in fact, and soon in name. Do you see?"

"It's a pretty plot," said the idiot. "But why, madame, do you—?"

"Say I'm a Christian—or say I'm jealous. My God! Shall I see him marry her?" That sounded as heartfelt as anything I had ever heard her say; real feeling throbbed in her voice. "Now go; but remember—this is what I have to tell you—that never, by night or by day, are you safe. Three men follow you as a guard. Is it not so? Well, three follow them; Michael's three are never two hundred yards from you. Your life is not worth a moment if ever they find you alone. Now go. Stay, the gate will be guarded by now. Go down softly, go past the summerhouse, on for a hundred yards, and you'll find a ladder against the wall. Get over it, and fly for your life."

Disappointingly, but not surprisingly, he did not flee. He had that greatest weapon of the ruling class: the smug prick didn't understand it was possible for him to lose.

"And you?" he asked Antoinette instead, as though they were there for a chat.

"I have my game to play too. If Michael finds out what I have done, we shall not meet again. If not, I may yet— But never mind. Go at once."

"But what will you tell him?"

"That you never came—that you saw through the trick."

He murmured something. I heard hasty footsteps and a rustle of skirts, and Antoinette said very clearly, "I want none of your kisses, sir. I want you to go."

He gave an easy laugh. "If you will not accept my homage—"

"No."

"Then at least know, madame, you have served the king well tonight. Where is he in the castle?"

Antoinette began to reply, voice low, then cried, "Hark! What's that?"

I had my cue, and stepped out from my hiding place, making plenty of noise.

"They're coming! They're too soon! Heavens, they're too soon!" Antoinette cried, then, "No, stop! You may shoot one, but what then?"

I had already guessed he would be armed, but it was a kindly thought of hers. I called out, "Mr. Rassendyll, we want to talk to you. Will you promise not to shoot till we've done?"

"Have I the pleasure of addressing Mr. Detchard?"

He sounded as though he thought he had scored a point. I have no objection to letting men have an inaccurate impression of their own superiority, so I said, sulkily, "Never mind names."

"Then let mine alone."

"All right, sire. I've an offer for you. Will you let us in? We pledge our honour to observe the truce."

"We can speak through the door. Stand outside and talk. Well, gentlemen, what's the offer?"

"A safe-conduct to the frontier, and fifty thousand pounds English."

There was a tiny silence. I knew, since Michael had ordered investigations, that Rassendyll had two thousand a year, which was a very handsome income and quite enough for a pleasant life. The sum Michael offered was obscene. "Fifty thousand," he repeated.

"Paid tomorrow, if you like. He is good for it; I have never known him fail to meet an obligation."

"It is a lot of money," he said, with temptation clear in his voice.

"It's the price of a crown. Take it, Rassendyll. Fifty thousand, your safety, and an experience few men have shared. You must know this imposture can't hold much longer."

"How do I know I can trust your safe-conduct?" he asked, and I thought, *We have you now.*

"You may not think much of my word," I said. "But you can trust self-interest. I don't want to die any more than you, and if this business comes out, we are all ripe for the axe. Michael would far rather return the Earl of Burlesdon's brother home, if that were possible, than have to explain his disappearance."

"That, I believe," Rassendyll said. "Well—"

I was on the top step, close to the door, leaning forwards. De Gautet and Bersonin were on the step behind me. Hence, I alone heard Antoinette whisper low, "He lies. Don't believe him. They are treacherous."

I could have cursed aloud. She went on, urgently, "Michael has told him to give you the money, then cut your throat and take it back. He is a killer. Don't believe him!"

Fucking hell, Antoinette, I thought, and hoped fervently that the other two had not heard.

"Well, it is a handsome offer," Rassendyll said loudly to me, in a tone that might have fooled a child. "Give me a minute to consider." He shuffled around a bit inside, evidently planning something.

I stepped away. De Gautet hissed to me, "You have failed. Let's kill him."

"Let's take him," I said. "He wasn't afraid of being overheard, so his companion must be at a distance."

A voice spoke from the summerhouse. "Gentlemen, I accept your offer, relying on your honour. If you will open the door—" Rassendyll suggested.

"Open it yourself," I told him.

"I can't. The latch has caught."

We could hardly stand here all night with him in the summerhouse. I gestured at the other two to keep him covered with their revolvers when he emerged, reached forwards and pulled the door open.

And the bastard came out at a run, hidden behind a great round shield. Three shots rang out and glanced off the metal, then Rassendyll ploughed into us, and we went down like ninepins. It was a wrought-iron tea table, I realised, as it hit me painfully on the hip. I swore and fired again, with no thought of capture now. My target was already running, but he took a snap shot behind him, and by pure luck the bullet scraped my shoulder. I went down again, as Antoinette shrieked my name. De Gautet sprinted after him; more shots were exchanged, and he came back cursing.

"He has reinforcements outside. We must hurry. Come on, Detchard, get up, and run!"

Michael dressed us all down in humiliating terms for our failure. My injury was hardly more than a scratch, but he ordered his doctor to put my arm in a sling, so as to give the impression I was less of a threat. I did not feel greatly like a threat as it was, having been caught by such a childish trick. One point to Rassendyll.

Michael gave hasty orders for the household to remove in case Colonel Sapt or Rassendyll decided to accuse us and perhaps Antoinette of a plot against the king. Antoinette was to travel by train, alone; I wondered if he was dangling her as bait for Rassendyll in some way. She had sabotaged Michael's best chance, getting me shot in the process, but there was no trace of guilt or fear in her face as she murmured her sympathies and goodnights before disappearing off to bed. I wanted to know what the devil she was up to, and found myself unreasonably angry with her interference.

It is a peculiar thing to be a double agent. I was here to serve Antoinette, I looked forward to getting my knife into Michael, metaphorically or otherwise, and yet after months in his service, I found it all too easy to think of *our side*, and forget my true mission in the urge to fight and win. The duke's party had the tricky job of all tricky jobs, and an impressive team to do it with, and I would have dearly liked to see if we could pull the business off for the sheer hell of it. I reminded myself severely that my purpose was not to make Michael king, and then spent the next hour with him and my colleagues talking about ways to do precisely that.

Michael said his people would put it about that I had been shot in a duel over a love affair, and named Antoinette as the lady. I retreated to my room to spend a slightly painful and very wakeful night wondering what the hell was going on.

CHAPTER ELEVEN

We regrouped in Zenda the next day, and Hentzau walked with me to see the king's accommodations.

"Made by order of Michael," he said, and gave me a smile that did not hold its usual carefree glee. It was a sunless look, and I asked, "You don't find work as a gaoler congenial?"

"I don't mind work, and I wouldn't mind holding a prisoner. This borders on torturing a lunatic. You'll see."

The drawbridge that formed the only access to the moated Tower led directly to a flight of stone steps going down below the general ground level to two small rooms, cut out of the rock that rose from the moat. The outer room was windowless, with three mattresses on the floor, and gave the only access to the inner room, which had one square window, a few feet above the moat.

Rudolf was held in the inner room. Hentzau entered, I with him, and said, "Good afternoon, Highness, and how are you?"

The king ignored me. He sprawled on the floor, his arms held close to his side by steel chains, which I could see at once were set into the wall too low for him to be able to stand. His face was pale and haggard, his eyes hazed with drink. The air reeked of wine and sweat, and the smell of a chamber pot inadequately cleaned, and of the burning torches, for the window was completely obscured.

"We keep him well sauced," Hentzau said. "He screams the place down for wine otherwise. I think it might kill him to stop."

"Do we allow him exercise?"

"No. Our master's command. He also commanded the chains."

"This is a foul game," I remarked. I do not claim I was moved— in my view, those who benefit from the trappings of kingship must accept the position's incidental risks, such as deposition and death, and I had no doubt of how Rudolf would have treated an enemy. But it was undeniably foul, and Hentzau glanced at me with a wry look and nodded.

"What is blocking the window?" I asked. "The air is thick."

"A pipe," Hentzau said. "Have you been told the plan? Take a good look then, and I shall explain outside. I need some fresh air."

He left Bersonin in charge and we walked some way into the grounds, where we could speak unobserved. We were silent until then, and when we had found a pleasant shady spot under a tree, he remarked, "You look a little drawn."

"Rassendyll shot me."

"I suppose he had good reason."

"Of course. This is a lot of fuckery, Hentzau, and I cannot see a way out of it. I have an increasing feeling that Sapt is not averse to the sight of Rassendyll on the throne. He makes a better king than Rudolf."

"That damned play-actor has been a spanner in the works from the beginning. He wouldn't take the money?"

"He was tempted, but no."

"I loathe people who don't succumb to temptation," Hentzau said. "What is the point of temptation otherwise? I share some of your apprehension, my Detchard, but I should tell you about Michael's plan."

"Go on."

"It's a double bluff. The supposed plan is this: The king is kept in the inner room. Three of us are to be in the outer room to defend the door in the event of attack. If it seems likely to be breached, one of us is to go into the inner room and cut the king's throat, then tie a weight, left conveniently there, to the body, and put him into the great pipe that now leads from the window into the moat."

"Have you ever lifted a body?" I demanded. "Especially one slippery with blood? We need a pulley there, if one man is to do it."

"Good point, for verisimilitude," Hentzau said. "Then, you see, those of us in the outer room will leave off fighting, nip into the inner room and simply slide down the pipe ourselves—waving to the dead man if we see him sinking, I suppose—swim round to where men with ropes will await us, clamber out of the moat, and come round to surprise the attacking forces from behind."

"Of course we will," I said drily. "It makes perfect sense. And for whose consumption is this ingenious idea?"

"Rassendyll's, of course. It is a greater temptation than fifty thousand: it promises the king's death at another's hand. While Rudolf lives, the play-actor's life depends on his. If Michael produces that wasted shell of a drunkard alive, he signs his own death warrant, but he also signs those of Rassendyll and Colonel Sapt. And if Flavia has accepted the play-actor's hand or is bearing his brat . . ."

"Rudolf alive is a weapon against every one of them. A last great act of malice that ruins all."

"Precisely," Hentzau said. "Whereas if Rudolf dies, and the body is lost forever, then Rassendyll can seat himself securely on the throne at the small cost of killing Michael. That is the bait: that we will kill the king for him."

"Therefore, we let the plan become known to Rassendyll and Sapt," I said, working it out. "Either they choose to let the true king rot in Zenda—a choice that could come back to haunt them—or they will be forced into an assault on the castle to save him."

"To save him, or to make sure he dies—which is necessary if Rassendyll intends to keep his arse on the throne and his cock in the princess. Either way, Michael hopes that Rassendyll will lead an attack. There can be—to the public—no good reason for the king himself to attack his brother's home, but it is within the true man's character. We kill Rassendyll and his men, Michael claims he had no idea his assailant was his monarch, a convenient doctor announces that Rudolf was maddened by drink, and the throne passes to Michael for lack of another candidate."

"What if Rassendyll doesn't attack?"

"Michael nurses the king tenderly back to health and produces him as a living j'accuse against Sapt, Rassendyll, and Flavia," Hentzau said. "He could present the entire thing as their coup. Who would believe, after all, that this doppelgänger just happened to be wandering through a forest at the right time? In Rudolf's current state, with Bersonin's little powders and evidence of a plot to replace him, I am informed it would be possible to confuse the benighted fool into believing that he was held in Sapt's dungeon and rescued by his brother."

I whistled. "It all sounds good, and God knows it's ambitious, but is it plausible?"

"I don't know. But the longer Rassendyll sits on the throne knowing the true king is dying by inches in Zenda, the greater his crime. I think the odds are he will attack here with the aim of eliminating the king and Michael together."

"You don't believe he will free the king and return him to his rightful place, then disappear into noble obscurity?" I suggested.

"Not for a second, no."

"Nor I. Well, we had best get ready to work."

"There will be plenty of that when the false king gets here, which cannot be long," Hentzau said. "I'd prefer to play."

"Well, I shouldn't want Jack to be a dull boy," I agreed. "My room, this night?"

"If we can work our way past Michael's moral guardians. I must say, it is pleasant to have you back here. I missed our conversations as well as our diversions."

I gave him a look. He laughed aloud. "Good God, you are suspicious. That was a compliment."

"I'm sure it was. I don't like compliments."

"Really? I love them."

"I should never have guessed, you wretched preening peacock. Do you want me to rhapsodise on your beauty?"

"I shouldn't mind," he said, with a sultry pout that was, irritatingly, effective even while it mocked. "Or you could just tell me how much you want my prick."

"Or I could speculate that you want mine," I said. "Does the thought of a sin as yet uncommitted send you into a frenzy of anticipation?"

"Is fucking a sin?" he tossed back. "I like to think it's a blessing."

"Don't ask me. I've cut too many throats to worry about sins."

"Well, let's say I want to eat every apple on the Tree of Knowledge. I should hate to die knowing there was an experience I missed."

"You may be in the wrong line of work, then, since I'll be impressed if we live to Christmas, as things stand."

"All the more reason to get on with it, then." He winked at me. "À ce soir, mon cher Jasper. Unless you want to tell me what's worrying you?"

"Our probable imminent demise? The king in his dungeon?"

He scoffed. "You don't care for that. Quite seriously, my friend, what is it? You have looked preoccupied since you got here."

"*Shot.* I look like I was shot."

"Oh, as if you care for that. I've seen your scars," he reminded me. "Well, don't tell me if you don't like. But you will speak if I can serve you?"

He sounded, for once, quite sincere. I nodded and left him sprawled there under the tree.

I have never been one for love as other people describe it, with grand passions and madness. I don't aspire to hold any man's heart or to be the first or only in his affections; I have never felt devotion, or the jealousy that so frequently accompanies it. The entire business sounds like an enormous waste of time, and though I had cared greatly for Henri, I had undeniably felt a certain relief once we had ended things. I simply do not care to possess or be possessed, and I do not apologise for this. The poets tell us that a great parade of passionate emotion is the sign of a higher and nobler constitution; I call it making a fuss.

But when I care for anyone, friend or lover—and that is not often—I care deeply. True companionship is a rare prize in a life like mine, where most people are, of necessity, disposable. That was why I was here for Toni, my friend, with her filthy grin and her unshiftable determination. Rupert of Hentzau was a beauty, a devil, a glorious fuck, a sharp wit, and all that was enjoyable, but I had not quite realised before this moment that I had come to regard him too as a companion.

And yet I had, it seemed, and I wasn't certain I should. I could not be positive he was trustworthy, or that he trusted me; I was entirely sure he was playing some game, but what and with whom remained a mystery. And since I was playing my own game, he was equally ill advised to extend his hand to me.

Neither of us ought to place faith in the other, in fact, and yet I could not help feeling we were both coming to do exactly that.

I decided not to think about it, just as I had been trying to avoid thinking about Antoinette, even if my features had evidently betrayed my worry. I now gave up that effort and returned to the chateau to find her. Since Michael was about some business, I suggested to her that we should take a walk.

"No, thank you."

"It will help my recovery."

She looked up with quick concern. "How is your shoulder? Jasper, I am so sorry."

"If only Rassendyll had accepted the offer," I said. "He wouldn't have shot me then. And do you know, I was quite sure he was going to."

Her eyes went wide. I held her gaze for a moment and then said, "Come for a walk."

We went out to the grounds, passing Hentzau, who gave Antoinette his usual burlesque bow. I took us a good distance away, yet remaining in full view of the chateau, and said, "Would you care to explain why you did that? Purely to queer Michael's pitch? If that tattletale Bersonin had heard, your life would not be worth a minute's purchase."

"Did he hear?"

"No, nor de Gautet. I'd have killed them both if they had. For God's sake, woman! I hope you know Rassendyll would have taken the offer if you had not interrupted."

"Yes, that's why I interrupted. I didn't want him to take it."

"Why not?"

"I don't want Michael to be king. Rassendyll stands in his way."

"I would like to point out that I was shot as a direct result of your sudden desire to play kingmaker," I said.

"Sorry."

"De rien. Do you think your chances of finding Lisl are better if Rassendyll wins this game of crowns?"

She didn't reply for a moment, and then she said, "Tell me something. Who do you think should rule Ruritania?"

"I don't care."

"In the abstract, as a matter of judgement of the candidates. Who would be best for the people?"

"I still don't care. None of them. Red Rudolf is best locked away; Michael is a bastard; Rassendyll is all piss and wind; Anders the republican is a dictator in waiting. None of them wants to rule for the sake of 'the people.' There is no *best*; there never is."

She took a few paces. Then she said, voice low, "I disagree. I think there is a better course for Ruritania."

"Once again, my dear, I truly do not care. I am not here for Ruritania and nor are you."

"No, I'm not. But . . . Do you know where I went last night, before the summerhouse?"

"A soirée, you said."

"That was the pretext. I went to speak to Princess Flavia."

"You *what*?"

"She asked me to serve her, to be her spy in Michael's camp. And I agreed."

"A spy for Flavia," I repeated somewhat hollowly. "Wait a moment. Does she know about Rassendyll?"

"For God's sake, Jasper," Antoinette said scathingly. "He's a different man, do you think she's an idiot? He hasn't admitted it to her, needless to say—he is all noble pledges of love and devotion, while he makes love to her under false pretences. And she in turn guards her ignorance very closely. Nobody must know that she knows."

"Why not?"

"So that she can 'discover' the truth when it suits her, and have Sapt and Rassendyll executed for treason."

"Ah. I see. Does she plan to?"

"Only if need be. She doesn't want Rassendyll dead if it can be avoided. Not yet, at least."

"Lucky for him. What does she want?" I asked.

"The throne, of course. For herself."

I was briefly silenced. Antoinette went on. "She does not want to be married to either of her cousins; she wants both Michael and Rudolf gone. Then she will marry Rassendyll in his pose as Rudolf V and have him appoint her queen in her own right, of equal status to the king in law, and she will rule with him as her puppet."

"And husband," I pointed out. "Might he not rule her?"

"I'd like to see him try," Antoinette said. "She will always hold the trump card over him. And once Michael is dead and the marriage made, well, Rassendyll can have an accident, and she can reign alone."

I considered that prospect—the smug Englishman reduced to a powerful woman's figurehead and bed-warmer—and found it pleasing. "I like her daring. In fact, I wish her all success. Does she need Rassendyll? If Michael and Rudolf were eliminated, would she not be the next heir?"

"No queen has ever ruled in her own right in Ruritania. The republican faction would call it an end to the monarchy if the male heirs died—or the Senate might summon some cousin, I suppose, and make her marry him. Whereas, if she were married to Rudolf—Rassendyll, that is—and declared queen, her power would be unassailable in private and public."

"Yes, I see."

"It's like chess," Antoinette added. "The queen can only win by removing the rival king and protecting her own."

"Rassendyll isn't actually her king, if we are to be technical."

"Red Rudolf tried to rape one of her ladies-in-waiting. She wants him dead."

I couldn't argue with that. "And you simply went to her and had this conversation at a soirée, over the tea table?"

"Hardly. She made a point of making my acquaintance when I first came to Strelsau as Michael's mistress, you know. She was kind, and told me to come to her if I needed help. I thought then that she was jealous."

"It sounds like she plays the long game."

Antoinette laughed. "Do you think I don't realise that? She has wanted me as a pawn all along. And I will be—while it achieves what I want. She has promised to help me find Lisl. She can arrange to have me watched and send a force of men when I next go to see her. She has so much more power than we do. And once I have my daughter, I will make Michael pay, and pay, and pay."

"They do say that, before you go on a mission of revenge, you should dig two graves," I observed.

"We'll need a lot more than two. Will you help me, Jasper? I have to fight for Flavia—it's my best chance—but I'd feel a lot happier with you on my side. I won't blame you if you leave; this is more than I can reasonably ask of a friend—but I am asking."

Flavia would doubtless be just as ruthless as any of the other candidates in cutting away loose ends should she win—perhaps more so. She could not be seen to act in the business; she would not have the power to protect her pawns openly for some time to come. To fight for her would mean staying to the bitter end, with no guarantees. I would have to be ready to flee with nothing but the clothes I stood up in, and hope they weren't too bloodstained.

On the other hand, Toni needed me, and it would be interesting.

"A proviso," I said. "Hentzau."

"Oh, you can't tell him," she said swiftly.

"I think he'll notice," I said. "He's the only man I'd fear of them all. And I don't think he loves Michael any more than I do. He's in it for the game, and this is a game few have played. To overthrow Rudolf for Michael, then Michael for Rassendyll, then Rassendyll for Flavia . . ."

"You're *smiling*," she said, in a decidedly smug tone.

"It's a hell of a thing," I said. "A damn fool way to go on. Oh, what the devil. Why not?"

CHAPTER TWELVE

I t is quite a confusing business to be a turncoat twice over, especially in the middle of such plots as were afoot at Zenda. If my honoured reader should ever consider playing the triple agent, I would recommend a notebook to keep track.

Almost as soon as I had returned to the Tower, Michael called us together to inform us all of the details of his scheme. Johann, his gamekeeper, was being fed the story about the plan to kill Rudolf. He would be used to pass that false information to the player-king's faction and, with luck, Rassendyll would mount an attack.

"Suppose we wrong him?" Hentzau suggested. He was peeling an orange as he spoke, its fresh, bright perfume an odd contrast to the heavy stone walls and general atmosphere of plotting. "Suppose Rassendyll truly wants to rescue the king?"

Michael scoffed. De Gautet said, drily, "The British sense of honour and fair play? Detchard, you are the expert on that."

There was a general murmur of mockery, to which I could scarcely object. I said, "I suspect all will depend on whether he is observed. I'm sure he has told Sapt and indeed himself that he intends to return the crown to its rightful owner. If he mounts a daring rescue attempt that causes us to cut the king's throat—well, he will say to himself, at least he tried."

"It's a good point, though," Michael said. "We shall let him know Rudolf's health is deteriorating, that he is like to die in captivity if his faction doesn't act."

"And we must install a pulley to lift the body to the pipe," Hentzau added. "Detchard has informed me of the difficulties of lifting a corpse."

"Quite right," de Gautet agreed.

"But we aren't going to have to lift it," whined Bersonin. "If Rassendyll comes in so far, we shall kill him."

"Nevertheless, verisimilitude is crucial," Hentzau said with solemnity. "That is the kind of detail that will give Johann's story credibility."

They went on discussing the matter; I sat back, considering what I might do. If I were a fanatic ready to give my life for Flavia, I would simply cut Rudolf's throat and then Michael's to leave the princess's way clear. But it would mean my death, since Michael was surrounded with armed loyalists, and I had no interest in dying for Ruritania, Flavia, or anyone. I thought, on the whole, that it might be best to let Michael's plan play out as it might. If Rassendyll attacked the castle, he would have to kill Michael, lest his imposture should be exposed. It would be easy enough then to get rid of the true king and leave Rassendyll triumphant and convinced of his own victory. It wouldn't do to have him realise that the business had been arranged by Flavia.

It would be more difficult if Rassendyll was truly bound on rescuing the king, and a thorough-going nuisance if the shiftless sod failed to take the bait at all, but we would just have to wait and see.

Michael rapped the table for my attention and moved on to his next piece of news. He had invited the Princess Flavia to pay a visit to Zenda, and at the same time caused Antoinette to write her a letter, of which he read us the text.

I have no cause to love you, but God forbid that you should fall into the power of the duke. Accept no invitations of his. Go nowhere without a large guard—a regiment is not too much to make you safe. Show this, if you can, to him who reigns in Strelsau.

"Rassendyll believes that Antoinette is his ally," Michael said complacently. "If he fears I will snatch the princess, he will be primed to fight even before Johann betrays our supposed plans to him."

"And if the princess is fearful, she will doubtless encourage him to do so," I added. "Perhaps Antoinette might write to her again if that is needed to prick Rassendyll into action."

"Yes, of course," Michael said impatiently, and there, I hoped, was an excuse if Antoinette should be found sending messages to Flavia.

When the meeting concluded, Michael held up a hand as we rose. "It is crucial that Johann believes the false story. He is told that three of you remain in the outer chamber guarding the king at all times. I will have him go down over the next day or so and see that with his own eyes. Therefore—"

"Are you suggesting we confine ourselves to that noisome dungeon for twelve hours a day?" Hentzau said, with some incredulity.

"Detchard, de Gautet, and Bersonin will go down now. Hentzau, Krafstein, and Lauengram will relieve them at seven o'clock tomorrow. Josef will bring you your meals. You will not leave your posts without my permission."

Hentzau gave a very audible sigh. Krafstein smirked at me. I resigned myself to an uncomfortable night in uncongenial company, and went to get a pack of cards.

Two days later, we had word that the king's party was coming to Zenda. By this point I had thoroughly cleaned out the pockets of both my forced companions, and we were all of us fuming from stale air, inactivity, and unwanted closeness. De Gautet's endless waxing of his moustachios, and Bersonin's unpleasant habit of viewing the king in chains and making taunting remarks, were as tiresome to me as being rooked at cards was to them, and I suspect much longer in that dungeon would have led one of us to do murder. But, as Michael informed me when I stood on the drawbridge to take a breath of clean air, the stage was at last set and the final act of the play was to begin.

The player-king's destination was the Chateau Tarlenheim, which was on the opposite side of Zenda town to the castle, about five miles further out. It is situated on rising ground above a large tract of wood; supposedly the king and his party were there for the boar-hunting. He was coming with Colonel Sapt and Fritz von Tarlenheim, to whose cousin the house belonged; in addition there were ten young gentlemen devotedly attached to the king. Allow me to quote Rassendyll's memoir on this:

They were informed that a friend of the king's was suspected to be forcibly confined within the Castle of Zenda. His rescue was one of the objects of the expedition; but, it was added, the king's main desire was to carry into effect certain steps against his treacherous brother, as to the precise nature of which they could not at present be further enlightened. Young, well-bred, brave, and loyal, they asked no more.

Imagine putting together a team of just ten men to assault a moated, fortified castle, and deciding their most important characteristic was to be "well-bred." What an arse.

Michael's spies had given us all we needed about who was coming from Strelsau, and the activity at Tarlenheim told us where they were going. Michael now sent Hentzau, accompanied by Krafstein and Lauengram, to begin the war of words by informing the false king that Michael and several of his servants lay sick of scarlet fever, an obvious lie designed to rouse his suspicions. He took the opportunity to charm the player-king, whom he had not met before—I never knew Hentzau pass up an opportunity to charm someone—and Rassendyll comments, *For my part, if a man must needs be a knave, I would have him a debonair knave, and I liked Rupert Hentzau better than his long-faced, close-eyed companions. It makes your sin no worse, as I conceive, to do it à la mode and stylishly.* This is perhaps the only topic on which I might agree with him.

That night Rassendyll headed out, muffled in a cloak, and took our watchers straight to an inn where he had stayed before and had made a damned nuisance of himself to the serving-girl. As it happened, she had an understanding with Johann the gamekeeper, and to Michael's intense satisfaction, Rassendyll charged her to bring Johann to him. He planned to subvert the very man that we had primed with false information to fool him. It summed up the whole affair in a nutshell.

Meanwhile Lauengram and two men went hunting in the woods around Chateau Tarlenheim, and managed to get a shot at one of Rassendyll's well-bred idiots who had gone for a wander alone at night. They winged him and sent him flying home with tales of murderous assassins in every shadow. That doubtless put the wind up the king's party nicely.

I had no part in the fun, instead enduring another uncomfortable night in an airless dungeon listening to the true king giggle and whimper on his bed of straw, and was thus not in the best of moods when the others came to relieve us. I worked off the frowstiness with a long walk in the morning air and then a fierce practice bout with de Gautet which came dangerously close to becoming a real swordfight, but I was still chafing for exercise when Hentzau sauntered up.

"Should you not be in the cellar?" I said, seeing no reason why he should be so fresh and cheerful when I was anything but.

"I have dispensation. Ride with me?"

"To where?"

"Chateau Tarlenheim. I have a message to deliver to the player-king."

"I suppose you're happy to play messenger boy."

"As happy as you are to play nursemaid and gaoler. Mount up, I want to ride."

It was a lovely day for it, bright high summer yet with a mountain breeze cutting through the heat, the warm air redolent of pine forests. We set out on the hillside route that skirted Zenda town rather than ride through its streets; I had had quite enough of people.

"You're chafing," Hentzau remarked after we had ridden in silence for a while.

"I don't like my accommodation."

"Or your employment?"

"If you will have it, no. Tell me something, Hentzau. You're a Ruritanian, born and bred. Who do you think should reign in Strelsau?"

He laughed. "He who can take the crown, of course. That is how monarchy works."

"I said 'should.' It's your country."

"Do you care who Britain's Prime Minister is? Do you even know?"

"Gladstone," I said. "Or Salisbury? One of the two, probably." They had been alternating for years; one lost track. "Anyway, we are not attempting to overthrow the British Prime Minister. Who do you think would make a good fist of ruling all this?" I gestured around me. We were riding on the high ground, atop the foothills of the mountains that ringed the country, with Zenda's prettily crooked red-roofed sprawl below, lush grass and wild flowers under our horses' hooves and birdsong in our ears. It was a landscape to make one think slightly less ill of poets.

Hentzau shook his head. "There's hardly a choice. Rudolf cannot even govern himself. Michael is a poisonous spider, but he has ruled his dukedom well. He might strive to be seen as a good king. Or he might let loose his self-indulgent temper and prove himself as bad as his brother, but there we are."

"What about the other candidates?"

"Rassendyll is in this game for himself. Anders of the populist scum is a vicious swine. And Germany is looming over the border. The Kaiser wants a military alliance, you know. Anders would like nothing better than to become a vassal state; Rassendyll would probably make an alliance with Britain instead and set himself up as Germany's foe. Michael has the edge, for me, of the four. Why do you ask, anyway?"

"I wanted your thoughts. What about Flavia?"

"Ruritania has not developed the habit of queens. You're asking the wrong man about all this, you know; I'm not political."

"Why do you serve Michael, then?"

"You should know."

"Should I?"

"How many lands have you seen, Detchard? How many adventures have you had? You live for danger."

"I live *by* danger. That is quite different."

"You love it, and you know it. I want action. Intrigue. I want . . ." He turned in the saddle, arms wide, indicating the world around us. "I want all of it. I want to live as though every day is my last; I want to fight for foolish causes and gamble everything on the turn of a card. I want never to set a guard on my speech or my thoughts. I want to take all the pleasure there is to take, and reach for more. I want to drown in bright colours and dance on the edge of clifftops. Of course I seized the chance to overthrow a king. Who would miss that opportunity?"

I reined in my horse abruptly and dismounted. "Get down."

Hentzau leapt lithely from his pretty mare. "Any reason?"

"Yes," I said, looping my steed's reins over a tree branch and reached for him.

He ducked away from my hands. "Uh-uh. First—" He secured his own horse and drew me along a few steps. Not up into the concealing trees, but towards the grassy edge of the hill, where the land was open to the skies. "And second, I want to know why you don't kiss. No; you have asked me all sorts of questions. I want to know."

"Why does it matter?"

"Because I like kissing," he said simply. "So I want to."

I contemplated him, curly hair dishevelled by the breeze, all shameless enjoyment. "It gives the wrong impression, and sometimes leads to expectations."

"O-oh. I see. But is that not your partner's fault, if they conceive unrealistic expectations?"

I tapped him on the nose. "No. If you do nothing else honestly in your life, fuck honestly. Otherwise you make intimate enemies, and that is the worst kind."

"I bow to your wisdom," Hentzau said. "In which spirit, and please don't take this the wrong way, I really am not going to cultivate expectations of you, and I should be deeply disappointed if you felt any of me. I want a great deal of you, but, shall we say, not in a regulated sort of way. I like to be free."

"Then we understand each other," I said, and this time when I reached for him, he stepped into my arms, hands coming up to cup my face, and kissed me.

It had been a long time. I had forgotten, or made myself forget, how much of pleasure lies in kissing, the soft slide of lips, the scrape of stubbled skin against stubbled skin—not that Hentzau had much use for a razor yet. Mouths meet, tongues tangle, fingers grip and slip and slide, all of it a connection so much more intimate than fucking.

And my God, Hentzau was a joy in my arms. He kissed with utter abandon, holding nothing back, apparently entirely unrestrained by the fact we were in the open air, albeit an unfrequented path. He kissed for his enjoyment and mine, and we staggered and stumbled our way to the ground, still kissing for the sheer glory of being alive, the wonder of finding a congenial soul in the world, and the very real prospect of being dead before the weekend.

Hentzau's fingers found the fastenings at my waist as I was fumbling for his. I had thought, if I thought anything, to expand his education, but I found I didn't want to cease kissing. The warm press of flesh, sun on my skin, and a tongue in my mouth was enough, each of us with a hand wrapped around both pricks, fingers entwined, rubbing up against one another like schoolboys, to a fast, effortless climax. I tipped my head back and groaned; he shouted aloud as he spent, a joyful yelp that rang off the hills.

"God, you're unsubtle," I said, once I had my breath back.

"Who cares for subtlety?" He kissed me again with a cheery *smack*. "See, is it not more fun like that?"

"Don't presume to educate me, wretch."

We lay there, enjoying the fresh air and birdsong, for a few minutes more, then Hentzau sighed. "I suppose we should get on."

"I suppose so. What is your mission?"

"To double Michael's offer. He is convinced he can buy Rassendyll off."

A hundred thousand pounds would buy most men. The player-king's disappearance would be without a doubt the best outcome for Michael, potentially allowing him to seize power without bloodshed; it would not at all suit Antoinette.

"I'd be sorry if you succeeded," I said aloud.

He twisted around to look at me. "Why?"

I might have told him then. But it was Antoinette's life at stake, and I am not in the habit of unconsidered confidences. "Oh, it would be a tedious anticlimax to events," I said instead, and he laughed and rolled away.

CHAPTER THIRTEEN

We rode together until we were close to the chateau, then I left my horse and went through the grounds on foot. There was only one guard posted, easily avoided; I prowled on until I came across Rassendyll sitting in the sun in an armchair, while one of his "hand-picked fighting men" played a guitar and sang love songs, and others sprawled around him at ease. Apparently the idiot thought he was on holiday. I settled behind a tree no more than twelve feet away, revolver in hand.

A few minutes later, as arranged, Hentzau came riding up the path. That, at least, got a reaction, the men scrambling to their feet. Hentzau dismounted close to the player-king, delivered a magnificently insincere bow, and requested private speech in order to deliver a message from the Duke of Strelsau.

"Withdraw," Rassendyll said, waving his hand at his men. "Yes, all of you. Go."

They went. Hentzau took one of the vacated chairs. "So the king is in love?"

"Not with life, my lord," Rassendyll said with a smirk.

"I'm sorry to hear it. If you'd prefer to die, that could be arranged."

The smirk disappeared. "That was to say, I am not so wedded to life that I would fear to lose it."

"Oh. Sorry. Yes, very good. Since we are alone, Rassendyll—"

The player-king drew himself up sharply, a picture of offended dignity. "I shall call one of my gentlemen to bring your horse, my lord. If you do not know how to address the king, my brother must find another messenger."

Hentzau gave him a pained look, withdrew a handkerchief, and removed a spot of dust from his riding boot. "If you insist. Although really, between ourselves, why keep up the farce?"

"Because I'm the king until any man proves otherwise," Rassendyll said savagely.

Hentzau inclined his head. "I bow to Your Majesty's honourable loyalty to his family."

Rassendyll's face reddened to the colour of his hair. "Is your mother dead?"

"What has that to do with it? Ay, she's dead."

"She may thank God. The world knows you broke her heart." He sneered, apparently considering himself to have struck a shrewd blow, and clumsy though it was, I saw Hentzau's nostrils flare. "Well, what's the message?"

Hentzau took a breath. "You do jump around. The duke offers you—"

"I doubt it will be enough," Rassendyll said. "I have the crown and the princess in my hand. What has he to offer me greater than that?"

"A choice," Hentzau said. "On one side, a bullet or a blade. Player-kings die real deaths, Your Majesty. On the other, safe conduct across the frontier and a million crowns. That's a hundred thousand English."

"I know what it is," he snapped. "It's not enough."

"I'm not here to haggle," Hentzau said. "In truth, sire, I'd prefer to see you dead than paid off. I'll tell Michael the offer won't do, shall I?"

Rassendyll's face darkened, but he could not now go back. "Tell him it is refused, as I should refuse any sum. Nothing would be enough to justify such a dereliction of my duty."

"Oh, was *that* what you meant? I'll tell him. Can I pass on any sentiments of fraternal love?"

"How is your prisoner?" Rassendyll retorted.

"The k—?"

"Your prisoner."

"I forgot your wishes, sire," Hentzau said. "I forgot you were the king now. Well, he is alive. And how's the pretty princess?"

Rassendyll snarled, and clenched a fist threateningly. Hentzau laughed in his face, and Rassendyll dropped his arm with an oath. "Go, while your skin's whole!"

Hentzau called the groom to bring him his horse, and dismissed the fellow with a crown. He made to mount, then paused and turned back to Rassendyll, who stood nearby, and stretched out his right hand, the other resting on his belt. "As we are gentlemen, then, let us part and shake hands."

Rassendyll sneered, put his hands pointedly behind his back, and bowed. The stupid prick. Hentzau's hand flashed out, the dagger glittering in it. I, having seen that coming a mile off, trained my gun on the oblivious "hand-picked gentlemen" even as the blade struck Rassendyll's conveniently placed and defenceless shoulder.

Rassendyll screamed. Hentzau wrenched the blade out, swung up onto his horse with magnificent grace, and was off at a gallop while Rassendyll's men were still disentangling their legs and shooting in random directions. I need not have bothered giving him cover at all.

I made my way out of the chateau grounds without difficulty— the man on guard, another tactical genius, had abandoned his post to run towards the commotion—and caught up with Hentzau at our designated meeting point. We rode at a pace too fast for conversation for a little while, until it became apparent that there was no pursuit, then settled back.

"What an arse," Hentzau said eventually.

"An idiot, too. You might as well have sent him a formal invitation to a stabbing. Remind me to teach you how to do that better."

"Thank you, I will. But I didn't particularly *want* to stab the bastard. I intended to annoy him, not to give him an excuse not to fight. I moved too enthusiastically."

"I've noticed you do that," I said, and the unusually grim look on his face softened to a grin. "I think you let him annoy you too?"

Hentzau exhaled. "Perhaps a little."

"If you've a weakness he knows, others may know it. You need to arm yourself."

"How? Do you feel nothing for your family? Could you hear your mother insulted?"

"My mother, myself, anyone. It's merely words. And I never greatly liked my mother."

"Well, I did mine," Hentzau retorted hotly, and turned his head away.

I allowed him a moment. "If you can be stirred to anger, you'll lose the fight."

"I know that, damn you!" he snapped, then took a breath. "I know. You are quite right. But— Ah, God. It wasn't just what he said, it was the way he presumed to think he knew. All the world presumes it. *Rupert Hentzau flaunted his mistresses in his mother's house. Drove her to her grave with a broken heart.* It is a damned insult."

I scarcely knew what to make of this. "Given the life you intend to live, you will hear a great deal worse insults, and probably deserve them all."

"Not an insult to me. To *her.*"

"That she died of a broken heart?" I asked, somewhat confused.

"She died of a disease of the lungs," Hentzau said. "She was married off to my father aged seventeen, when he was forty. He was old-fashioned, which is to say a brute. He circumscribed her life to nothing more than church, nursery, and drawing room, and would not let me go to school. We were all to live in his house forever, the shutters half-closed, no light, no air, puppets in his domestic dollhouse. She told me stories, though. She bought me books and hid them; she engaged tutors with imagination; she insisted I should learn to ride and secretly paid my instructors to teach me how to use a sword. I was seventeen when my father died of an apoplexy, and I thought we would both be free at last, but she was already ailing by then. It took her three years to die, and in all that time, she begged me to live for us both. She wanted the house filled with pleasure; she asked me to introduce my mistresses, and laughed at their stories, and made me promise not to marry early—as if I had not had quite enough of the domestic hearth—and she lived for tales of the life she had never been permitted to have. Broken heart, indeed. My father was the one who crushed her, not I, except that she would not be crushed. She refused a priest when she died, you know. She told me she'd had enough of God for an eternity, and laughed till she coughed blood."

"I see where you get your character from," I said. "Embrace the insults, Hentzau. Let people believe they know your weakness, and they will be weaker for it. Personally, I like nothing more than an opponent who suggests I am less of a fighter because of who I fuck. That tends to make them delightfully overconfident."

"Oh, I see that. But even so— No, you're right. I do know. But I don't like it, all the same."

I didn't tell him, *You'll get used to it*. He would find that out for himself; the world would not be his playground forever. He sighed. "Thank you for listening to me. I am a fool to let a fool bother me."

"You are, rather. Still, at least you stabbed him."

"Yes, there's that," he agreed, cheering up. "Come, let's ride. I dare say Michael would like to know how his message was received, and I want my lunch."

(I may note here that Rassendyll's account of the same meeting casts himself in a significantly more heroic light, and has him winning the battle of words. One would expect nothing else.)

Michael was not best pleased about the results of Hentzau's embassy and packed him off back down to the cellar, while he growled around the castle making himself unpleasant. He could not bear the waiting, and I began to wonder if he felt guilty too. He had given the orders for his brother to be confined without air or exercise, fed with the drink that rotted him from within. It was a miserable and unnecessary cruelty—a foolish one, too, for nobody would now believe the wretch in our cell to be the same man as the healthy, sun-kissed Rassendyll. Michael had placed his lifelong spite above his own interests and common sense, but although he hated Rudolf, the man was still his brother, and a king. Antoinette reported that the duke slept poorly, and woke with incoherent cries. Conscience doth make cowards of us all, or so they say; I've never troubled much with it myself.

The watches were exchanged briskly that evening. I sat on a straw mattress playing solitaire since my companions did not care for cards any more, until a hasty pair of boots clattered down the stone steps. It was Krafstein.

"Johann is headed in the direction of Tarlenheim. He goes to meet the false king!"

"The filthy traitor," de Gautet said, although this was exactly what we had intended Johann to do. "He deserves the severest punishment."

"You already killed his mother," I pointed out. Possibly I had been spending too much time with Hentzau. De Gautet glowered at me, and I hauled myself up. "Well, if he is gone out then we need not continue this farce."

"The duke wants it maintained," Krafstein said. "At least for tonight. We cannot have Johann learn by accident that this was for his benefit. After he returns, he is to be flogged on some excuse, to ensure his loyalties are thoroughly given to Rassendyll's party, and then we shall await action."

"It can't come soon enough," I retorted, but I lay down on my straw mattress once more, planning the next move. I had to speak to Hentzau and let the cards fall as they might. If he was determined to fight for Michael, we might find ourselves battling in earnest; even if I managed to avoid that, he had irritated the player-king too much, and was without question guilty of the grossest treason. Let Rassendyll triumph, and Rupert Hentzau's head would be the first to top a spike.

I didn't want to see that (although since my head would probably be up there as well, the issue would be unlikely to arise). He was a ridiculous, preening, vulnerable, arrogant young fool, and the world was a more entertaining place with him in it. I did not want to watch him march gaily to destruction. I would have to trust him with the truth, which meant my life and Antoinette's, and pray that my absurd sense of companionship with him was not leading me astray.

Johann returned late that night. He was given a flogging for immorality in staying out so late courting, and to season his resentment was told that it was on Hentzau's orders. Hentzau, who had almost every possible fault but was at least no hypocrite, was inclined to be indignant about this.

Johann was sent down to his keeper's hut the next morning to nurse his wounds in disgrace, which freed us from the tedium of constant mass watching of the outer room; shortly thereafter we were brought the news that the king had been seriously wounded with a spear while hunting boar. What an unutterably manly excuse. Michael returned the favour by letting it be known to Johann that he believed the wound to be serious, and so the smoke and mirrors went on.

Meanwhile I resolved to speak to Hentzau.

It was easier said than done. Michael, whose fears grew alongside his hopes and whose eyes were always distrustful now, had us all going over the Tower and its surrounds, ensuring we covered every inch of ground, considering possibilities for assaults. De Gautet and I had the most experience of warfare, and we were yoked together for much of the day while Hentzau had his own tasks. Around five that evening I finally tracked him down in the Tower, where he was checking Bersonin's pulley, watched with a sort of dull blankness by the king.

"A word with you, when you can," I said.

"Certainly. Now if you like?"

"Upstairs."

He gave me a waggle of the eyebrow, gave the pulley rope a final tug, and said, "That'll hold. All right, carry on."

"Do we need it to hold?" I asked, leading the way up. The Tower had many rooms and more passageways; it was a sneaking, creaking sort of place, and I looked around as we went to be sure we were unobserved. I should have preferred to go out in the open grounds where eavesdroppers could not lurk unseen, but to be inaudible would have made us all too visible, and I did not want to be too obviously seeking private conversation now. I had walked alone with Hentzau often enough, but treachery makes a man self-conscious.

"We might want it yet," Hentzau answered with a shrug. "I can imagine circumstances in which two dead King Rudolfs would be inconvenient. Or two live ones, come to that."

I drew him into a side room, one with a single entrance and that through a second chamber. It had no lock, but I preferred to have the warning of approach, and would not have cared to explain why two of the duke's loyal men had locked themselves in for a private conversation. He gave me a puzzled look. "You seem somewhat serious for a dalliance."

"I am serious, and I'm not dallying. Hentzau, listen to me. We've spoken of this business a few times now. I think I'm right in saying you're no great devotee of the duke, and we both know he has no guarantee of success. How would you feel about changing your allegiance?"

His brows drew together. "Do you propose I switch sides in the hope of saving my skin? Because I doubt that Rassendyll would accept me on his side if I presented him with the crown on a silver salver. And if I were afraid, I shouldn't have embarked on this game."

"On the contrary," I said. "I thought you might like to make this twice as difficult and three times as dangerous."

He was a couple of inches shorter than me: not much, but noticeable this close. He looked up now from under those dark brows, with a smile that Satan himself might have worn before he started his rebellion. "You interest me strangely. Go on."

"I take Flavia's side," I said, barely above a breath.

"Flavia," he repeated.

"Think of it. If she has Rudolf and Michael out of her way, and Rassendyll at her side but under her thumb—"

"That, I grasp," he said. "But how do you come to this position? I wasn't aware you were devoted to Ruritania's best interests."

"I don't give a fuck for politics. I am here—I have always been here—to help my friend."

"Your— You don't mean de Mauban?"

"Herself. We are old acquaintances. She set up my employment here. Michael has taken her daughter and keeps the child hidden, using her to make Antoinette obedient. She is not yet two, his own child, and he threatens to send her to a brothel."

"What a prince he is."

"I came to see if I could help Antoinette. I have failed, but now Flavia has said she will find the child."

"She's recruited de Mauban," Hentzau said. "Well. *Well.*"

"You understand, I hope, that if you fuck with Antoinette in any way, including betraying this confidence, I will gut you like an eel."

"I take it you're closer than I knew."

"Not lovers, if you mean that, but she saved my neck from the guillotine once. She is dear to me, and she wants her child, and her money, and to see Michael dead. I have not been able to help her with the first, but Flavia will—in return for her allegiance. So . . ."

"Very clever," he said. "Oh, very. Detchard—"

"No, listen to me now," I said. "There are three people I care to see come out of this business with a whole skin, and none of them is named Elphberg. If you and I work together, I think we can do this. And in truth I don't want to fight you. I'd prefer to be on the same side. I think we could pull this off and come out of it alive, with Antoinette too. We'd have to run like hell afterwards, naturally, but you said you wanted adventure."

"I did, didn't I. And what an adventure. To unseat a king, undermine Michael in his own stronghold, and put an impostor on the throne—"

"It's a game as large as I'll ever play," I said. "Are you with me?"

"Betraying king and duke alike, with no reward but a cut throat if we are discovered?" Those dark eyes were fairly blazing now. "To the ends of the earth. But, Detchard, listen—"

I held my hand up as he spoke, and we both heard the sound at once: a whisper of foot on stone. We had been speaking low enough that only voices, not words, would have been audible, but it was the two of us, huddled alone in secret conference in the Tower, where only Michael's most loyal men set foot. I could think of only one reason other than treason why we should be so closeted, and Hentzau leapt to the same conclusion. He grabbed my face, I grabbed his arse, and we were very satisfactorily tangled together and humping shamelessly against one another by the time the stealthy watcher had crept to the door.

And, so far as I could tell over Hentzau's dramatically breathy moans, stayed there. The door's planks were somewhat warped, with cracks between; someone evidently liked to watch. I put a mental wager on Bersonin.

Hentzau was as aware as I we were being observed; his response was entirely predictable. He wrapped a thigh over mine with a provocative grind of his hips. "Jasper, oh Jasper," he groaned. "I cannot resist you; I must submit. Fuck me, you beast of a man. Take me now."

I wasn't sure whether to laugh, hit him, or do precisely as he had requested and see how he liked it. I did not have to decide, because the door opened sharply, and a voice said, "Well, then."

It was not Bersonin. It was Michael. Whoops.

I believe the correct form for guilty lovers discovered is to spring apart. I can't say we did. Hentzau sighed with dramatic exasperation and made no effort to disentangle himself. I gave his arse a firm squeeze before releasing it, and said, "Your Grace. How may I serve you?"

Michael's eyes narrowed. "Better than this, I hope."

"There's really nothing else to do until the play-actor bestirs himself, my lord duke," Hentzau pointed out, with a negligent yawn. "So we must find ways to occupy ourselves, just as Your Grace does with his own charming companion. Sadly, the rest of us have no ladies to whom we may turn, and unless Your Grace is generous enough to share—"

"Is there something that requires my attention?" I put in, hoping to shut him up.

Michael contemplated us for a moment, then gave a smile. "Well, I dare say you might as well amuse yourselves while you have the leisure. But not on duty, please. You will kindly accompany me now; I have business for you."

We followed him down the stairs. Behind his back, I gave Hentzau a questioning look. He shrugged. It seemed a peculiarly considerate and relaxed approach from Michael at a time when he was twitching with nerves, and I could not help but wonder if he had heard our words after all. I was soon to find out.

CHAPTER FOURTEEN

I was hard put to seem unconcerned for the rest of that day. I knew Michael was watching us, and at points in the afternoon he slipped away to speak privately with the others of the Six. Hentzau appeared entirely lighthearted, but he was good at that. I settled for grimly uncommunicative, a demeanour I could carry off well thanks to years of practice, and made sure I had my concealed knife ready to hand. If our plotting had been overheard, our lives would be forfeit. Well, that was always part of the game, but I intended to take Michael with me if I possibly could.

We were, as I have said, all housed in the chateau, Hentzau on the first floor in one of the guest rooms, I on the second, in the much less elegant quarters usually reserved for serving-men. That evening the Six (with the exception of Lauengram, who alone guarded the king) dined within the chateau, Michael at our head. He poured wine with a lavish hand—you may believe I watched his hands and Bersonin's, and did not drink until the others did—bidding us be good comrades, and inviting Hentzau, in particular, to grow offensive. "Come, tell us more about de Gautet's moustaches!" he cried, and laughed, and refilled his glass again.

I didn't like it. I didn't know what he wanted, but I didn't like it, or this false carousing, still less the way Michael watched Hentzau with that little cold smile on his lips.

Michael looked set to drink all night, and keep us with him, but as the clock struck ten he shook his head and stood. "Enough, gentlemen. We must all be sharp in the morning. To bed."

"A word, Detchard," Krafstein requested as I made to leave. I stopped. He drew me to one side and smiled at me. "Merely an observation from the duke. As of tomorrow, we will all be standing watch on Rudolf once more, so you would be well advised to seize the day. Or rather, the night."

I turned on my heel without response, not entirely sure what to say. It seemed implausible that Michael was concerned with my desires at all, still less that he had chosen to bestow his blessing upon us. And he had made a point of getting Hentzau drunk.

Hentzau had gone on ahead. I therefore went down a passage that led both to a jakes and to stairs up to my room, and as I walked down the corridor, a hand from a shadowed doorway gripped my arm. I seized it and was close to breaking the wrist before I realised my assailant was Antoinette.

"Ow!"

"Sorry."

She glared at me. "Brute. Jasper, do you intend to go to Hentzau tonight?"

"Why is everyone in this castle obsessed with my bedroom activities?" I demanded.

She jerked me close so her words were barely audible. "Because there are spyholes in the walls of all the rooms on the first floor. And Michael uses them."

I will freely admit, that floored me. "The devil he does."

"He can see, and he can hear too," she said, eyes meeting mine, and she did not need to spell out that warning. "And he likes to watch. He will be watching. So will I, I expect."

"Charming," I said. "I shall disappoint him by going to bed. Hentzau's drunk, and I'm not paid to perform for Michael Elphberg."

"Jasper, he doubts Hentzau," Antoinette said softly. "And now he doubts you. Be careful."

We both looked around at the sound of footsteps. Antoinette moved back into the alcove of the door. I reached for my dagger, but relaxed when I saw Hentzau, looking damp. He had apparently tipped a jug of water over himself, because he seemed alert and his eyes were bright.

"Jasper. I wondered where you had got to. And—" He gave Antoinette a magnificent bow. "Thank you for waylaying him, my dear. I have a use for our stern swordsman this night."

"Hentzau—"

"Shh," he said, putting a fond finger to my lips, and mouthed very clearly, *Shut up.* "Indulge me. Eat, drink, and be merry, for tomorrow we die. Milady, as an expert yourself, and since you constantly refuse to fuck me, will you not persuade this puritan Englishman to do so instead?"

"I wish he would," she said, voice clear and teasing—professional, in fact. They were watching one another like cats. "Jasper, take advantage when it's offered. Even better, convert him to the joys of man-flesh for good and the ladies of Ruritania will have cause to bless your name. I am to bed—and not with you, Hentzau. I am meat for your master."

She walked off down the corridor, head high, and as she turned the corner I heard her say, "Oh, good evening, Herr Krafstein. I had not seen you there."

Hentzau rolled his eyes expressively and tugged at my arm. "Come on."

I went. He was evidently a great deal less drunk than I had thought, or than he had chosen to seem. We strolled through the corridors arm in arm—Krafstein had disappeared—with Hentzau chattering airily about nothing, and went up the stairs, making our leisurely way to his room.

There was nobody about in that corridor. I seized him, pushing him against the wall, and kissed him forcibly. He responded with all the enthusiasm I would normally have hoped for, and a great deal more than I wanted at this moment, almost to the point of distraction, his lips hard and hot against mine, body unquestionably eager. I pulled my mouth away from his and bent my head to lick at his neck, then worked my way up to his ear, and murmured, "Spyholes in your walls."

"Yes, yes," he panted.

I grabbed both hands and pulled his arms over his head, pinning him against the panelling and leaning in. He was definitely enjoying this. "Are you listening to me?"

"Mmm." His gaze met mine for a flicker of a second, enough to convey that he had understood.

I leaned in hard against him to murmur, "Just pass out drunk."

He twined a thigh through my legs, pressing forwards against me, nuzzling my cheek and neck, and said low, "Not a chance. Unless you're shy?"

He was making a thoroughly wanton display of himself, arched and panting, which I had no doubt was deliberate, but he was also very hard, and the sparkle in his eyes was not counterfeited. Now I thought of it, it came as no surprise whatsoever that the little peacock liked to be observed. God knew he was worth watching.

I shoved him back against the wall and growled, audibly for our listeners' benefit, "What do you want?"

"You said you could make me beg for it. Well, make me."

Good God. "Under Michael's eye?"

"He'll love it. It will prove I've nothing else on my mind. And I want it, Jasper." He said that for my ear, not our listeners'. "I really . . . very much . . . do."

His foot was raking the back of my calf, the boot heel digging urgently in. I hauled him away from the wall and said, "Come on, then."

I have, myself, no objection to being watched as such. I don't consider fucking a sacred act—it is hard to when one is liable to be gaoled for it—and I had spent most of my life in boarding school, the Army, and the more insalubrious back streets of half a dozen cities. Privacy is a privilege; I have frequently not had funds, or time, or safety to secure a quiet room with a bed and a lock. So I do not mind being watched. I *do* object most strongly to being spied upon as a matter of general principle, but the fact that we knew made some small difference.

Not nearly as much difference as Hentzau's eagerness. He was flown with wine but more so with gleeful anticipation. I knew several men who found observation doubled their pleasure, and now I thought of it, Antoinette had said Hentzau liked more than two in a bed. Evidently my young devil was not of a private nature, and who was I to argue.

We stumbled into his room. I had not been in it before; it was finely furnished, suitable for a gentleman of birth. My main concern was for the bed, which was large with posts but no hangings. I supposed Michael did not like his view obstructed. I pushed Hentzau onto the bed and came down on top of him, and we kissed savagely and hard, biting and rolling, making frankly something of a spectacle of ourselves. Well, if the duke liked to watch, he should have a show.

We broke off to disrobe, I standing, Hentzau sitting on the bed. He began pulling off his clothes at speed again, the heedless boy. I waited till he had stripped to the waist, then said, "Stop."

"Why?"

"Shut up. Lie back."

He did so, extended over the bed, chest bare, looking up at me with gleaming eyes. We were both dressed in the Ruritanian fashion with tight buckskins and high black riding boots, polished to a sheen. Ah, Rupert Hentzau and his boots. I stood by the bed, looking down.

"What are you waiting for?" he enquired.

"You'll work it out."

He opened his mouth to say something annoying, which became a gasp when I pinched a nipple hard. "Ow. *Ow.*"

"Does that hurt?" I squeezed harder. He yelped. I ran my nails over his skin, down his side, returned to graze the nipples again until I had tormented them to hardness, slapped him when he squirmed. "Lie still." I slid my hands down those taut, buckskin-covered legs, and up between them, over the muscular thighs until he jerked, and slapped him harder, for sound rather than pain. "Don't move until I tell you."

"Why not?"

I slid my hand over his calf, encased in smooth leather. "Once you have your boots off, I'm going to fuck you. But not until then."

"Perhaps we could take them off, then?" he suggested.

"In due course. I'm enjoying myself. I'm going to enjoy myself very thoroughly with you, and you are going to please me."

"It seems that you're pleasing me," he managed, sounding slightly strangled as I ran my hand all the way up one smooth leg and over the bulge of his crotch.

"Give it time," I suggested and went to work.

I had wanted a full night with him, and I made use of it. I caressed and licked and bit, roaming his body with my hands and mouth until he was moaning without restraint, shoving him down every time he tried to wriggle or squirm. "God's sake, Jasper!"

I skimmed my hand over his straining crotch, making him buck. "I said, still."

"How the fuck am I supposed to lie still?" he yelped.

"Try," I said. "Don't move at all. Be a good boy now; it will be worth your while."

He swore at me, gritted his teeth, and stilled. I didn't think I had ever seen that before; he was always toe-tapping and squirming and on the move. A restless youth, my Rupert, but a determined one. He held still, and I slid my hands over and under him, stroking the curve of his arse, the join of his legs, the bulge of his arousal, over and over until he said, "*Please.*"

"Please what?"

"Please do something before I spend like this, damn it!"

"Wrong." I rubbed him gently with my palm. He whimpered. "I will keep you like this as long as you need to learn. Please what?"

He thought about it. "Please take my boots off?"

"Better. Not quite good enough, though."

He made a strangled noise. "What then?"

I sat on the side of the bed with some awkwardness, easing off my own boots slowly and carefully. Rupert watched, eyes huge and dark in the candlelight. I had no idea if Michael was still watching, and in truth couldn't give a damn if he was; still, I was careful not to let the hidden knife fall when I shed my own clothing, and dropped my buckskins close by the bed where I could reach for the weapon if I needed it.

I knelt naked, straddling Rupert's chest with my full weight and pinioning his arms with my legs. "Persuade me."

"Am I allowed to move?"

I took hold of my prick and gave it a long stroke. "No."

Rupert licked his lips. "Then what—?"

"Ask."

"Take my boots off and fuck me?" Rupert suggested, adding, "That is, if you would be so kind?"

"Wrong again. You learn slowly."

He made a determined effort to buck me off, which would have worked with a smaller man. I planted a heavy hand on his chest, over the base of his neck just below the lovely hollow of his throat, and saw his eyes widen.

"Rupert," I said softly. "Do you recall me saying I would teach you to give?"

"Mmm." His skin vibrated under my fingers with the sound.

"This is the first lesson. If you merely take, you must take what is given to you. It's not just about what you want."

He thought that one through. "What do *you* want?"

"Try harder."

"All right: how may I please you?" I cocked my head. He shut his eyes. "Would you care to fuck me at all, Jasper? If that would please you?"

"Eventually." I shifted to get one hand behind me, massaging his arousal. He whimpered. "When I'm ready."

"May I help you get ready?" he suggested, running a tongue over his lips in a pointed fashion.

"I think we'll get you ready instead," I said. "Stay still, now." I shifted back off him and eased up one leg. He lay with head thrown back, looking like one of the more salacious religious paintings. I picked up his calf, stroking the boot and the leg above it till his breathing was harsh, then eased the boot off. He gave a groan of relief.

"Not yet," I said. "Stroke yourself. No, leave that button where it is. As you are will do very well."

Rupert blinked, but obeyed, running his hand over his trapped prick. He watched my face. I watched his, and saw his eyes darken. "More."

"I—" He bit that off. "Do you like that? Watching me do this?"

"Very much."

He slowed his movements, making them firmer, teeth set against the threat of climax. "Whatever you say, then."

I could barely breathe, for all the bravado. I wanted to make him spend like that; I wanted him bare; I wanted him spread out for me and moaning. I waited just a moment more until his hand and breath were quickening, and then said, "Unbutton yourself."

His fingers shook as he obeyed, drawing out his rigid prick, shining with soft moisture. It was irresistible. I bent forwards and took him in my mouth. He moaned pleasure, hips twitching in his effort to stay still, and I sucked him deep into my mouth, once, twice, and let go.

"Jesus!" He spasmed on the bed. "Jasper!"

"You can come with me inside you. Not before. Would you like me to take your other boot off?"

He whimpered agreement. I grinned. "Then stroke yourself. But don't spend."

"May—not be possible."

"Make it possible."

He set his teeth, giving his prick the slightest, most tentative stroke. I shook my head. "More. And harder. I'll fuck you when you want it enough. Show me that."

Rupert exhaled, hand moving with more certainty, wrapped around his cock. His lips moved slightly; I imagine he was doing Latin declensions in his head. I certainly was. I took hold of his boot. "Don't stop, now."

I took my time working the boot off. Rupert whispered an oath. "Right. Buckskins," I told him, and he let go of himself with a gasp of relief. He looked painfully hard. I eased the tight trousers down his legs, stripping him bare, and knelt over him, looking my fill.

It wasn't that he was a beauty. That catches my interest but doesn't keep it. It was the pure unrestrained, unashamed, bursting life of him, the way he flung himself into whatever he did with utter commitment. For most of us, living is simply our ongoing state until we die; Rupert lived as an active verb, and did it as hard as he could. I had absolutely no doubt that he would have played the master with me every bit as enthusiastically so long as he got to play, and having an audience only made it better.

I slid my hands over his bare thighs, stroking his flanks, staying just a little away from his straining prick. He groaned. I took both his wrists, pulling his arms wide, and leaned forwards over him, weight heavy on his wrists, trapping him under me. I dare say I looked intimidating, all scars and sinew; it was certainly my intention, and I made my voice accordingly harsh. "Are you ready to give me what I want?"

Rupert looked up at me, all huge appealing eyes and soft unresisting body, playing the helpless youth for all he was worth. It was irritatingly effective given that he was as defenceless as a cobra, and I don't like helpless youths anyway. "Oh, yes, Jasper," he said. "Please—"

"Uh-uh," I said. "No more asking. I'm going to fuck you for my own pleasure, and you are going to take everything I do. It's all about what I want now. Understand?"

"Whatever you want," he echoed breathily, submissively, with the candlelight striking sparks from his eyes, and I gave up on finesse.

"Turn over," I told him. "No, a moment." Shit; I had not had this in mind today. One can manage perfectly well without lubrication or without experience, but not without either, and I wanted my Rupert's first time to be memorable for the right reasons. "Oil. Linseed will do well. Have you any? Then fetch it."

I clambered off him; he hopped up and retrieved a bottle from a chest. "Excellent. Lie down."

He lay, face down, legs spread. I poured oil into the palm of my hand and went to work.

That night is a cloud of impressions in my memory. I recall the candlelight, the warm glow and flickering shadows, the way it turned Rupert's skin mellow gold and lit the smooth planes of his back, the smooth shifting of his muscles. I recall the way his body tensed, just briefly, and then opened to me, how he twisted around my fingers, his wordless yelps, the way he pushed back and whimpered, and the almost unbearable building need, so that when at last I pushed into his body—still so tight—I feared I would spend at once. And Rupert, writhing and groaning, breathing through the initial pain with a fighter's disregard, finding his point of pleasure with a laughing, surprised inhalation that almost undid me.

Christ, he was a marvel. I wrapped my arms round him, fucked him and stroked him, brought him off crying out his long-delayed ecstasy, and then pushed him face down on the mattress, holding his shoulder down, and took my own enjoyment, knowing how much he would feel every stroke now. He cried out my name, muffled in the sheets, as I fucked him, and I cried out his, unable to stop myself, when I came.

Rupert, my Rupert. Reckless and wary, graceful and graceless, handsome, debonair, vile, and, for just one night, very thoroughly conquered indeed.

We lay together afterwards, awash in sweat and spending and the smell of fucking, entwined with one another in a way I would not normally encourage, and in which I would not have indulged with another man. There is so much comfort in closeness and bare skin, so much peace to be had in lying together. The chance had rarely come my way; if one even has the privilege of a bed, one is all too often obliged to hop out of it to avoid the objecting landlord or the avenging law (whatever it might be avenging). And I had not done well by my last lover: I did not, in truth, deserve peaceful embraces. But Rupert gave his body, his affection, with such absurd generosity that I let myself take both in the same spirit, and sank blissfully into that brief moment of rest.

I wondered if Michael was still watching, the spying, lying prick. I hoped he'd had as much enjoyment as we.

CHAPTER FIFTEEN

It took Rassendyll two days to act. Perhaps he delayed because Princess Flavia came up to Tarlenheim; perhaps her presence was what spurred him to act at all. I didn't know, and if Hentzau did, he didn't tell me.

The day after that memorable night was a trying one even to a man of as few sensibilities as myself. Michael kept us busy from dawn to dusk, and had us split up once more to guard the king, with Hentzau and I on separate shifts. And he had evidently drawn conclusions from his secret spying: he said nothing so far as I know, but he looked at Hentzau with a little contemptuous smile. That was entirely predictable, and indeed I was sure Hentzau had wanted to provoke precisely that response as a means of deflecting suspicion, but it rankled nevertheless. I have no patience with the idea that a man's courage or competence are related to his bedroom habits, and I knew an urge to slap that smile off Michael's face, but masked it. Hentzau and I would settle our score with Michael Elphberg in due course, and it would be a grand reckoning indeed.

There was a summer storm the night Rassendyll attacked. I was in the Tower, guarding the king. I had the windowless outer room to myself, since Bersonin and de Gautet were stretching their legs up and down the stairs. The drawbridge was up and the Tower as close to impregnable as might be, except for the great pipe. I had pointed out that a daring man might climb up inside it, and Michael had been chewing on that ever since. His solution was to moor a boat by the pipe and set men to spend the night at watch.

Max, the manservant, was on duty. It is hard enough to stay awake on guard duty on one's feet, there was no sense of urgency in his mind, and he had covered himself with a warm oilskin against the rain. Of course he slept.

I didn't hear it when Rassendyll cut his throat in the dark. I heard nothing at all until the first shots rang out, and then I drew my sword and held myself poised to act.

If the attack was coming, I would need to kill de Gautet quickly, since he was unquestionably the greatest threat. Rassendyll would doubtless be able to cope with Bersonin. He could heroically fight his way through and—if I did not mistake my man—take a moment to ensure the king was found dead on the straw. I intended to use the pipe for my way out, concealing myself in the dark water until someone friendly lowered a rope, and then go after Michael.

So I readied my blade, checked my pistol, and positioned myself by the closed but unlocked door, prepared to take de Gautet when he ran in to defend the king.

But the attack did not come. There was more gunfire, more shouts, and then nothing. After a few moments, footsteps came down the stairs. "Detchard! Don't shoot—it is I, de Gautet. Open up."

"What's happening?" I asked, making scraping noises with the bolt.

"An attack. As far as I could see from the window, Krafstein is hurt and perhaps Hentzau. The assailants have ridden away, it seems, but we must keep close guard."

I sheathed my blade and opened the door; Bersonin came down to join us, and the three of us watched and waited in silence.

Hentzau perhaps hurt. Well, a minor blooding would teach him caution, and if his wound was more serious, there was nothing I could do about it. So I stood with my uncongenial companions, impatient and alert, through the rest of what proved a very long and entirely uneventful night.

Morning came with the usual call from the chateau signalling that the drawbridge was to be lowered. I will admit I was pleased to see Hentzau standing on the other side of the moat, apparently in rude health. He crossed the bridge as soon as it had swung into place and held his hand up as the three of us emerged, herding us back within the Tower.

"What's afoot?" I asked him.

"Excursions and alarums last night. Krafstein and Lauengram are dead. And Max, too, the manservant."

I whistled. "Rassendyll did well."

"I got one of his men and Lauengram two before he fell, so honours are even." Hentzau had a look I recognised, that glittering spark of excitement that comes only from life on the edge of death. "It was a close thing with me, come to that."

He was clearly desperate to give the story, and it made me remember how young he was. I said, "Come, tell us what happened."

"The king's party attacked by stealth last night. One man ahead with a number of others on horseback. Michael had sent me, Lauengram, and Krafstein to ride down to Zenda—"

"In the middle of the night, in a storm?"

"He had a task for Krafstein, and asked us both to accompany him," Hentzau said. "Except we did not get so far, because we were just riding round the road when we heard a whistle and the sound of horses. We rode up, shouting to raise the alarm, and there was a melee. There were perhaps ten of them, all told. Lauengram fought damned bravely, but he fell, and Krafstein too. We had put paid to three of them by then but there were plenty left, I alone in the middle of it, and I heard the king—the player-king—shout my name and cry, 'Shoot! Shoot!'"

"A nasty position," I said. "Mind you, they don't seem to have shot particularly well?"

"Not well, but a great deal," he said, narrowing his eyes at me, and entirely failing to hide their sparkle. "I took my brave Hilda—my mare, you know—round as close to the moat as I dared, and leapt in."

"You jumped into the moat from horseback?"

"If I'd kept riding, they'd have kept shooting and they'd surely have hit Hilda," Hentzau explained. "I threw myself in and swam like the water was filled with sharks, with bullets dropping around me. Cursed dark and cold it was, too. I called for help, and after what I can only call an unconscionably long delay, more of our side came running up, and someone hauled me out. By then the king's party had long gone. They threw the bodies into the moat first—Krafstein and Lauengram, and even Max, though his throat had been cut in the boat. The player-king was the one who assassinated him, by the way; he was soaking wet."

I whistled. "He's got more spine than I would have guessed."

"He's certainly a force to be reckoned with against a sleeping man," Hentzau agreed. "I did not have the chance to engage him directly myself."

"And the Six are down to four," de Gautet said. "I regret our companions. We shall doubtless have an opportunity to avenge them."

"Michael wants close guard kept now," Hentzau said. "He wishes to speak with you all. Although that would leave the king with only your humble servant as protector, a fact I fear he may have forgotten. Detchard, stay with me. De Gautet, do me the service of advising His Grace that we stay to guard his brother."

In the face of such cheek, de Gautet and Bersonin merely bowed and withdrew. Hentzau escorted them to the Tower door, locked and bolted it, turned to me, and said, "I killed Krafstein."

"An interesting manoeuvre while outnumbered in a fight. Any reason beyond his personality?"

"You are enraging," Hentzau said, with some vigour. "I tell you I murdered one of the Six and that is all you have to say?"

"What do you want me to do, congratulate you? Well done on a successful assassination. Stop playing the fool and tell me why."

Hentzau gave me a mock-glower which in no way hid the fact that he was relishing every moment. If ever I knew a soul born to walk the edge, it was he.

"As I say, I killed him in the struggle, once we had set about Rassendyll's men. Lauengram fought damned bravely, but I saw him go down under two swords at once, one to the chest. It struck me as a good opportunity to deal with Krafstein too. We can better control the situation with fewer actors on the scene."

"Probably true, as long as you weren't seen," I agreed. "I conclude that you have taken my side, then?"

"I have done no such thing," he said. "I was trying to tell you this before Michael interrupted us the other day. You've taken mine."

"I beg your pardon?"

"You know perfectly well I'm no lover of the duke," he said. "I'm surprised you didn't see it yourself, to be honest. I'm Flavia's man. Have been all along."

I stared at him. He gave me an absurd grin compounded of bravado, amusement, and a hint of "dog wondering if the master likes large dead rats after all."

"You're working for the princess?"

"In her interests, certainly."

"Since when?"

"Since before I got here. It's why I came. She spoke to me months ago, when I was still drinking with Rudolf; it was she who suggested I switch allegiance between the brothers so that I could play spy in Michael's camp for her."

"But— Is that what you were doing with those surreptitious trips to Zenda?"

"Mmm. I don't think I managed that any too well; I didn't realise how suspicious Michael was. And then I was meant to seduce de Mauban to Flavia's side by whatever means necessary, but you wouldn't let me get near her, so on the whole I haven't been a great deal of use, really. I suppose you were looking for clues to de Mauban's child when you were burgling his rooms?"

"Failing to burgle. Yes. Oh, for Christ's sake. You really might have said. If we'd known back in the lodge, when this started—"

"Believe me, that has occurred to me more than once. I thought you were loyal to Michael, so I acted accordingly."

"As did I. God damn it," I said. "Fine. Can't be helped. And have you a grand plan of which I should know?"

"Not at all. I have not received any messages from Flavia recently."

"Antoinette may have. You and she should speak. Hentzau, tell me this: if Flavia wins, will you be safe? As her man, I mean?"

"Not at all, no. She told me she will not protect me at risk of her own character, and her hand cannot be seen in the business. If Rassendyll wins, I shall have to fend for myself. You look stern; why? She is a woman of her word, and she doesn't make promises she cannot keep. I knew what I was getting into, my Detchard."

"I'm sure you did. And you do it for the joy of being a nuisance?"

"Do you know, I'm not sure," he said thoughtfully. "Because it's adventure, yes, and in a lady's name. But—don't laugh, will you?— I think it's possible I do it for Ruritania too. You asked me what I thought a while ago, and I told the truth so far as I could. Well, the full truth is, I think Flavia will bring fresh air to a country that sorely needs it. She has ideas, where the brothers Elphberg have never wanted the crown for any reason but to prevent the other one from getting it. I think the whole world is changing, and we need to change with it, and not by sliding into vassalage with Germany or Britain either." He gave me a laughing shrug. "For heaven's sake, don't tell anyone I'm a patriot, will you? It would ruin my reputation, and I really don't plan to do it again."

"I doubt you'll have the chance once your head has been removed," I said. "Well, I shall keep your altruism secret if you don't tell anyone I'm doing all this for the sake of a baby."

"That is quite sickeningly sentimental," he agreed. "Here's to ruthless mercenary callousness."

"Quite. I'll speak to Antoinette and let her know," I said. "She may be able to communicate with Flavia, or serve as a go-between if Michael insists on keeping you and I apart."

"Tiresome bastard that he is. Excellent. And, Detchard?"

"Mmm?"

He gave me a wry grin. "Thank you for trusting me. With you on my side—"

"You're on *my* side."

"Either way, I really couldn't ask for a better companion in treason. I begin to feel reasonably positive."

"Your optimism amazes me," I said. "Speaking of plots, we should ensure we look sufficiently dishevelled when we emerge from here. For verisimilitude."

"Verisimilitude is my great goal in life," he agreed, and stepped into my arms.

The hostilities of that night inevitably drew a certain amount of attention from the general public. Rassendyll had lost three of his well-bred men, and Lauengram was of a noble family. Duelling was a commonplace in Ruritania, but not at such a high and deadly rate, and people shook their heads over this renewed outbreak of factional hostilities between the king and his brother. Accordingly, the player-king issued a grave statement condemning the violence, and a public apology to Michael for the loss of his men. Michael returned an even more fulsome apology, and both sides existed in a state of inaction for a few days as the public tutting died down. This dancing around what was, in effect, a civil war may seem absurd, but both Michael and Rassendyll had far too much to hide, and neither could afford to face close examination of his actions.

We shipped Krafstein's body back to his family, but Lauengram's elderly mother requested he be buried by the duke, his master. Michael therefore arranged a sombre procession, which was to pass through Zenda (and with luck inflame feeling against the king's men). The coffin was placed on a funeral carriage drawn by four black horses, and Hentzau and I were tasked to accompany it. De Gautet and Bersonin guarded the king; Michael kept up his pretence of scarlet fever.

The procession wound its way down the hill as slowly and tediously as these things always do. I rode behind Hentzau but could not benefit from the view, as I had my eyes straight ahead in the correct show of respect, which meant that they fell on the party of riders at the bottom of the hill: a red-haired man and a red-haired woman, both finely dressed, along with a stout military man and a bevy of attendants. I heard Hentzau give a quiet hissing laugh.

Rassendyll sent a groom over to our party. He exchanged a word with Hentzau, who halted the funerary procession with a wave of his hand and beckoned to me. We rode up to the player-king together.

Rassendyll had a good seat on a horse and looked well enough in his borrowed plumage, a bright blue military-style coat. He appeared somewhat garish to my mind, especially next to Rupert of Hentzau's sombre magnificence in a black frock-coat, but perhaps that was only my partiality. I was significantly more interested in the Princess Flavia. She was pale and composed, dressed with elegance and restraint, red hair pinned up, nothing given away. She looked between us all, and her eyes met mine.

Hentzau gave the king's party a low bow. "Your Majesty asks whom we escort. It is my dear friend, Albert of Lauengram, slain in a contretemps with—well, it would be tactless to say it."

"Sir, no one regrets the unfortunate affair more than I," Rassendyll replied with equal insincerity. "My ordinance, which I mean to have obeyed, is witness to it."

"My condolences. The poor fellow," said Flavia. It was not a particularly heartfelt statement, but Hentzau bowed again as though she had poured out her soul with tears.

"Your Majesty's words are gracious," he said. "I grieve for my friend. Yet, sire, others must soon lie as he lies now."

"It is a thing we all do well to remember, my lord," Rassendyll snapped back.

"Even kings, sire," Hentzau added sententiously. "Even kings die."

"It is true. How fares my brother, my lord?"

"He is better, sire. He hopes soon to leave for Strelsau, when his health is secured."

"He is only convalescent then?" Rassendyll asked.

"There remain one or two small troubles bothering him," Hentzau returned with a flashing smile.

"Express my earnest hope that they may soon cease to trouble him," Flavia said. Her tone was again unemotional, and both Hentzau and Rassendyll turned and bowed to her.

"Your Royal Highness's wish is, humbly, my own," said Hentzau. "I bid your majesties good day; we go on sadder duty."

We bowed and turned our horses, but a moment later Rassendyll hailed us back, and came trotting up, unaccompanied. "One more word with you, Hentzau—apart."

Colonel Sapt was glaring at the pair, with one hand on his revolver. I glanced at Hentzau, who nodded, and I fell back as he and Rassendyll rode aside. I nudged my horse to take me in a circle as though she were ambling freely, and was not at all surprised when Princess Flavia came up to me.

"Mr. Detchard," she said. "I believe you and I have friends in common."

I bowed, something I do with a great deal less grace than Hentzau. She gave me a warm smile. "Let's not waste time, shall we? De Mauban tells me you stand by her. She has a means of contacting me, if that is necessary. Are you willing to serve me, Mr. Detchard?"

"I am willing to act for Antoinette," I said. "I'm not one for service."

Her eyes narrowed. "And why do you stand with de Mauban rather than your master or your countryman—or me?"

"I put friendship above country, a very long way," I said. "Ruritania's affairs are not my business. And I have a bone to pick with Michael Elphberg."

She nodded, as though a hired murderer might reasonably have a quarrel with a duke. "And your goal in all this? What is it you hope to win?"

"Antoinette and her child together and safe across the border. If you do your part in achieving that, milady, I'll do mine."

Her look was somewhat dry. "You don't ask for reward, or for indemnity? I'm a little old to believe in the kindness of mercenaries, Mr. Detchard."

"I'm not doing you a kindness, madam, and as far as I'm aware, you're not offering indemnity. So Hentzau tells me, at least," I added. Not that I doubted him as such, but one would be a fool not to check.

"I am not," she said. "I offered that young man something of much greater value to him."

"An adventure?"

Her lips curved. I had had a feeling she wouldn't be entirely immune to his charm. "Quite."

"That works for young men. As for me, I owe Antoinette a debt. If you will find her daughter, you have my hand on her behalf."

She considered me, face intent, then gave me a pretty, smiling nod of the head, by which I deduced that Rassendyll was returning. "The work is afoot. If it is in my power, Mademoiselle de Mauban will have her child; certainly she will have my protection whatever may befall. I give you my word on that, as an Elphberg and a woman." There was just a slight flare to her nostrils when she said that, and I wondered if the princess had fellow-feeling with the courtesan. Being destined from birth to wed Red Rudolf might make something of a suffragette even out of an aristocrat.

I bowed my thanks. She nodded. "Go well, Englishman."

I bowed again, aware of other eyes on me, and took myself off to the somewhat neglected funeral cortège, passing an exasperated-looking Rassendyll on the way. We maintained decorum all the way to the church, and through the service, which was mercifully brief and sparsely attended, but did not trouble to hold our positions on our return to the castle.

"What were you talking to Flavia about?" Hentzau asked.

"She assured me that she will keep Antoinette safe, and throw us to the wolves without compunction. Tell me about Rassendyll."

"He offered me money and safe conduct to bring him the king alive."

"I doubt you could manage it, and I don't believe in his safe conduct for a minute."

"No, nor do I. In any case that was merely an opening gambit for negotiations. I suggested instead that we plan his attack on the castle together."

I choked. "You what?"

"Well, it makes sense. I told him that he should arrange the time of the attack with me, and I will make sure Michael is killed and Rudolf disappears."

"And why would he believe that was a genuine offer?" I asked, with some exasperation.

"Well, I told him I wanted a free hand with the lovely Antoinette," Hentzau explained. "That she only has eyes for Michael, who is cursedly in my way. So if I could remove him—"

"—she would immediately fall into your arms over the corpse of her lover? Even Rassendyll couldn't believe that."

"I don't think he's concerned with her opinion," Hentzau said. "The point is that with Michael dead, there would be nobody to protect her from me. I think I made it plausible, and I asked for money too. He cursed me roundly, but he's thinking about it."

"It's a risk," I said. "Michael has always felt uncertain of you. Suppose Rassendyll decides to sow dissension by revealing your double dealing?"

"Well, he may. I hope Flavia will encourage him to more dramatic action, though. And if we could direct his plans, it would be worth a great deal."

"True enough," I said. "Be careful, though. Michael is a jealous brute, and if you show interest in Antoinette, she's likely to be the one who suffers for it."

"She knows that," Hentzau said, with the laugh in his eyes for once absent. "She and I have spoken, and she'll play her part like the rest of us. Chivalry doesn't become you, Detchard."

"I look to my friends."

"Your friends can look to themselves. I want Michael to believe in my interest in de Mauban, and she is happy to let me proceed. And if I catch you attempting to wrap me in cotton wool, you and I will fall out."

I raised a hand. "Noted. I will simply observe that, if your interest is real, you should know that Antoinette eats boys like you for breakfast, and picks her teeth with the bones."

Hentzau gave a shout of laughter, wildly inappropriate for his sombre dress. "I can well imagine. I would love to find out, I admit—not now, but once she has regained control of her destiny. Should you object, do you think?"

I found myself pleased that he had asked. It suggested an interest in continuing our association which I found unnervingly welcome. "As you say, she can look to herself and so can you. And I claim no right over your affections. You may do as you please—so long as it pleases Antoinette, needless to say—and so shall I. But I appreciate the courtesy."

Hentzau grinned at me. "My morals may be lacking, but I do try to maintain my manners."

"It is amazing to me how those are the first thing to go in any affair," I remarked. "I don't need fidelity, or adoration, or extravagant vows. Those are all will-o'-the-wisps. Whereas good manners require effort."

And so we rode on, talking for all the world as though we were not two murderers in the process of committing treason at a funeral, and I can only say, that is what Ruritania and Rupert Hentzau do to a man.

CHAPTER SIXTEEN

Rassendyll's next move—or possibly Flavia's—took the castle of Zenda entirely by surprise. With the pair of them still in Tarlenheim, it was given out that a date had been set for public solemnisation of their betrothal. This ceremony is near as binding as marriage under Ruritanian law, and it would be celebrated in Strelsau cathedral in a fortnight's time.

Michael reacted furiously. He was sure now that Rassendyll intended to steal the throne in plain sight, and he felt helpless to object. His mood was not improved by Hentzau's reaction, which was to wish Antoinette joy on a rival gone, and observe that the princess had, on the whole, probably made the best choice. Michael cursed him in the foulest language and informed me that I should keep my catamite under control. Hentzau laughed in his face and kissed Antoinette's hand; she slapped him with such force that any man might have been convinced except I. When Antoinette really intended a slap to count, she turned her rings inwards so that they drew blood.

All told, it was Happy Families in the castle of Zenda as we waited for the endgame.

Johann, the treacherous keeper, had been informed that the king lay gravely ill and would surely be dead already were it not for Antoinette's tender nursing. Words fail me. But he believed it, and took that message back to Colonel Sapt. This presented the impostor with a clear choice: he must attempt to rescue the king, or openly decide to let the man die. I don't know what went on in Tarlenheim then, and Rassendyll's account is not worth the paper it's written on, but at last the player-king made his choice.

The protection of the true king was this. I and Bersonin were set to watch by night, Hentzau and de Gautet by day. We were all billetted in the Tower now: the two not on duty were supposed to rest in a room by the drawbridge entrance, within sound of a cry. Because of the Tower's inconvenient medieval layout, this room was a few stairs above ground level and across the hall, and one had to go down and through the door by the drawbridge to where the king was lodged. The four of us all had keys to the king's dungeon.

Michael still lodged in the chateau. He had commanded the drawbridge to be raised at night, only to be lowered on his command, thus cutting the Tower off. It had doubtless seemed a clever stroke a few years ago to change the drawbridge so that it was lowered from the chateau side, turning the Tower from a secure fortress into a prison, but that alteration now meant that, if the chateau were conquered, those inside would be trapped by the moat and unable to flee, while the invaders could simply let the bridge down and walk in. I suppose Michael was happy to ensure that the Tower's defenders would fight to the death. Having no such intention, I had secured my strong black cord in an unobtrusive spot of the moat, on the far side from the chateau, in case Hentzau or I needed to climb out. I hoped it would not be found, and that it would be strong enough to take our weight.

Antoinette also remained in the chateau, but was now locked in at night as soon as she returned to her own apartments opposite Michael's—for her safety, Michael told us, and cast a malevolent look at Hentzau's cheerfully lecherous demeanour.

That was the set-up, and we had now only to wait for Rassendyll to mount his attack.

"He will come at night and in secret," Michael said. "And when he does, we must treat it as an attack of bandits. Extinguish the lights, fight in the dark, kill all you can and shout all you can over any voices. We will smear the faces of the dead with lamp-black. How can I be blamed for defending my home against assault? How could I know that the king himself was part of a larcenous criminal attack in the middle of the night, while my people slept? Nobody can blame me if he is killed on an unprovoked midnight raid on my castle."

"The question of the prisoner may arise," I suggested. "It is murmured that you hold a man in the dungeons, and people may conclude that the player-king attacked to free him."

Michael smiled. "There will be a man in the dungeons. Hentzau, I think, will do me that service. It will only be a few days in chains without rations to give you a suitably worn appearance. Then the false king's party may explain why they raided my property to release a man with whom Rudolf is known to have fallen out. We will suggest they had more sinister intentions towards him. And nobody will deny my right to chastise my own gentlemen."

Hentzau looked as though he would have very much liked to deny that right, but he said only, "A charming scheme," with an ironic bow. There was no great point in objecting, when we had no intention of letting Michael get so far.

It was not, in truth, a bad plan. There could be no reasonable explanation for a king raiding his brother's house in the night, and so long as Michael's forces won, he would be able to claim that he did not recognise his attacker until too late. This did, however, mean that the castle at Zenda could not be put on a military footing: it was crucial that Michael did not seem to be expecting the king's attack. Instead he had the word put about that gangs of bandits had been seen close to the border and roaming into Ruritania, and he ordered that the servants who always slept in the front hall should be armed with pikes. That was a risk, since Rassendyll's men would doubtless carry guns, but it would look better than replacing them with trained and properly armed soldiers, and Michael tended to consider his servants as disposable.

His main concern was not, in fact, the chateau's security but the king in the Tower, since he calculated Rassendyll would have no choice but to make that attempt himself to hide his secret, and one of the four of us waiting there would be able to put a permanent end to his adventurous career.

"So Michael will be innocently defending himself in his chateau, while the king is accidentally killed in a separate building," I observed to Hentzau. "Which is to say, if public opinion demands that a head should roll for the 'accident,' it won't be Michael's."

"I wonder how many of us he intends to leave alive, if he becomes king," Hentzau mused.

"Bersonin, to kill the rest. And once he's done that, he won't be long for this world."

"A fine reward for service."

"Well, we won't get any better from the other side," I pointed out. Rassendyll would want the remnants of the Six, along with Michael and probably Antoinette, dead in order to keep the secret of his identity. It would be child's play to give him a victory and the crown without him realising that was our aim, but how we would do it and get away with our lives was less obvious. "Have you any news from the lady?"

We were in the Tower as we talked, since Hentzau was on duty, in one of the higher rooms, looking out over the moat at the chateau. We spoke in hushed tones with the door shut, but I still had no intention of naming Flavia aloud.

"None. I suppose your friend has heard nothing either?" I shook my head. "What will you do if the attack comes before you know about the child?"

That was the question. We still had no idea where Lisl was and no word from Flavia on the subject. That worried me for two reasons. If Flavia had not kept her promise, then we could not trust her word for Antoinette's safety. And Michael was the only man who could tell us where Lisl was held: if he died in the hostilities, I was concerned that we might never find her. Anyone who had carried out his casual cruelties under orders would melt away once Michael was no longer there to protect them, and Flavia would have greater and larger tasks ahead of her than finding a whore's bastard.

"I'll have to ask our master, I suppose," I said. I didn't know if I could force the information out of Michael at all—he was just the sort of obstinate swine who would lie under torture out of spite, and I doubted I'd have leisure to work on him in any case, but I could think of nothing else to do. That meant keeping him alive in the teeth of Rassendyll's attack and Flavia's wishes, which made me a quadruple agent by now, and I could not hold back a laugh at the thought.

"I'm glad you find this amusing," Hentzau said. "I'll be fighting for my cause, you know."

"And I for mine. I hope they will prove to be the same."

"So do I," he said. "It strikes me that we may not get many more opportunities to talk, my Detchard. I feel I should say—"

"Uh-uh. No goodbyes," I said. "It puts one in the wrong frame of mind for a fight. And if we are separated, I shall expect to find you via the Hundsstüberl inn."

"On Kazmairstrasse in Munich," he agreed. "I remember my lesson, schoolmaster. I didn't realise you were an optimist."

"I haven't died yet, and I don't intend to start now. Do you?"

"Not if I can help it."

"Then there's no need for sentiment."

He gave me a sideways grin. "Clearly not. I will simply observe that if—when—we do meet again in that inn, I hope it will have a large bed and a sturdy door."

"A bottle of good red wine too. And then you can put your lesson of the other night into practice."

"The lesson in how to reduce a man to a whimpering heap and then fuck him senseless?"

"That very one."

Hentzau looked me up and down with appreciative assessment. "I'd like to try my hand at that. Do you think I could make you beg, Jasper?"

"We'll find out, won't we?"

"Yes," he said. "Yes, of course we will."

I think that evening was the first time in his life my reckless Rupert had really understood that he would die one day and that it might be soon. I'm glad I was with him then; it is not a pleasant awareness to reach on one's own. I had no great faith in our chances either, needless to say, but at least I was used to it. So he stood by me in silence, and after a moment held himself straighter, and I knew he had conquered that natural sense of creeping anticipation that can nibble away so unpleasantly at the will.

We looked out of the window together, in lieu of saying any of the things that would not help either of us in our resolve, and that was why I saw the flag.

"What's that?" I said aloud.

"What?" Hentzau asked, then, "That red cloth in the chateau window, you mean?"

It was Antoinette's window. I knew the signal from the brothel where Toni and I had met: the whores would hang up a red scarf or shirt as a way to attract attention without screaming. "Excuse me," I said, and set off down the stairs at a run, pausing only to snatch up something I had been reading as an excuse.

I had to stride, rather than run, when I got to the drawbridge, to avoid attention. I headed into the chateau and up the stairs to Antoinette's rooms, hand casually on my hip where I carried a knife. Her door was unlocked, and I let myself in without knocking.

Toni was there, alone, apparently unharmed. I looked to her for a sign, and she gave me a sharp nod.

"Mademoiselle," I said. "I have brought you that book I mentioned." I held it out, in case we were observed.

"*Care and Construction of the Chamelot-Delvigne Service Revolver*," she murmured. "Thank you, Detchard, how thoughtful. Is there a happy ending?"

"Unfortunately not. It turns out the hero was a double-action revolver all along."

"The cad." She drew me over to the window as she spoke, voice very low, and switched to demotic French in case of listening servants. "I had a letter from Rassendyll, via Johann. You know that I have sent him messages begging him to save me from this den of murderers. Well, he has replied at last. He wants me to scream rape against Rupert Hentzau tomorrow night, at two in the morning."

I took that in. "The idea is to draw Michael out of his apartment, to protect you?"

"Yes, so I suppose."

"That will be the time of the attack, then. Michael will be bent on revenge against Hentzau, Rassendyll's men will presumably attack then, all attention will be drawn to the chateau, and I dare say the player-king will take his opportunity to slip into the Tower and do what he needs. A pretty distraction. Have you given the letter to Michael?"

"Not yet," she said softly. "And it is the first letter from Rassendyll, and Flavia tells me he has used a wound on his hand as an excuse not to write. Michael won't know his handwriting. Does he know yours?"

"I doubt it. I haven't picked up a pen in months."

Her eyes met mine. "Rewrite the letter," she said. "I must have a paper to hand over to Michael, just in case he decides to interrogate Johann, but set the date for two days hence instead of tomorrow. The attack will come the day before Michael expects. Rassendyll can take him by surprise."

"What about Lisl?" I asked.

She set her jaw. "I trust Flavia. I *have* to trust Flavia. I have no choice."

"I could put a knife to Michael's throat and ask him."

She shook her head. "And what then? Kill him and wait for Rassendyll? Or flee, breaking my promise to Flavia, with the knowledge we both carry, and no guarantee Michael told you the truth? What then? I can't take the risk. Write it, Jasper, please."

"Wait," I said. "It occurs to me that Michael will guess your treachery very quickly, if your distraction and Rassendyll's attack take place exactly to plan but a day early. Let us at least change the scheme a little. If I write that you are to, say, set a fire, then Michael will not expect to hear you cry rape. It may keep him from realising you have double-crossed him a little longer." Probably not long enough, I thought, and wondered how fast and how good Rassendyll's men might be.

Toni exhaled. "I didn't think of that. Thank you."

I sat and wrote. My hand bore a reasonable resemblance to Rassendyll's; I suppose we had both had the same public-school training. He had made no effort to disguise his meaning except to write in French. That, I feared, did not bode well: if the player-king was ready to leave incriminating documents around, it was probably because he intended to silence their holders.

I blotted the letter and took the blotting paper to burn later. "You realise that this will put you in the firing line. As soon as Michael realises you have betrayed him—"

"I know."

"He has the key to your door."

"I know."

"At least put a chair under the door handle."

She gave me a look. "Do you have a knife to spare?"

I handed her the blade I carried. "Can you use it?"

"I don't know. I've never tried."

"Then you can't."

"I really do want to stab him. That will surely help?"

"Not enough," I said. "I'll think of something. You won't be alone."

"Will you not have sufficient on your plate?" she replied tartly.

"I'll think of something," I repeated. "Will you keep the original letter or shall I?"

"I will."

I didn't tell her to hide it carefully. She didn't tell me that it would be no use as a bargaining chip if it was carried on my cooling corpse. We both knew.

"Very well," I said. "Take care, chérie."

"You too. Bonne chance," she said softly. "To both of you. Tell Hentzau I'm sorry I slapped him."

"It's good for him."

"Oh, he needs taking in hand." She grinned at me. "Which, may I say, you did magnificently. Michael was—"

"I don't want to know what Michael was. Did he have you watch that?"

She fluttered her eyelashes. "It was the most fun I've had in this castle for a long time. You've matured well. When we get back to Vienna, you should consider taking up the whip professionally."

"Thank you, my dear. I prefer the knife."

"That's why you'd be marvellous with the whip, of course. That edge of danger, which is so delicious when it's—it's not—"

"Not real," I finished, when she could not. "I know."

"I'm frightened, Jasper," she said softly.

"I know you are. And nevertheless, you will bring Michael the letter, and play your part, and we will all do what we can. I'm sorry I couldn't do better."

She grasped my hands. "You've done all you could. You've been a pal, mon cher. And we'll meet again, won't we?"

"We will. Courage, my dear."

"Always." She put her head up high. I squeezed her hands, and let go, and then I took my book and walked back to the Tower, and left my friend to carry off a lie on which her life, and mine, and those of many others would hang.

I found Hentzau back in the Tower and murmured the news into his ear. He considered it in silence for a moment. "Tomorrow night."

"Yes."

"Michael will be angry, and de Mauban unprotected."

"I want to talk to you about that."

Hentzau nodded, then looked round as someone from the floor below called my name. "Later. Good fortune, Jasper. And—"

I pulled him to me, kissed him once, hard, and released him. He gave me a rueful smile. "That too."

CHAPTER SEVENTEEN

The next day was slow to the point of agony. I made sure I slept, and ate well, and exercised lightly to keep my muscles warm. I checked my weapons over and made sure I had my sword to hand, my belt knife, my concealed knife at my back, my boot knife, and a loaded revolver. I don't like to be unprepared.

I barely saw Hentzau, who was in the Tower all day; I did not see Antoinette.

Bersonin and I relieved Hentzau and de Gautet that evening. They went over to the chateau; we settled down in our usual silence. I had no desire to speak to Bersonin, and as he wandered over to make snide observations to the chained king, I knew a strong hope that he at least would not survive the night.

I have not spoken of the king a great deal. I have no desire to think of him after those endless days guarding his cell, listening to his shouts and orders degenerate into pleas and muttering. It was an unclean business, and had it been up to me I should have given him a swift death weeks before, but then, I have never aspired to be a king. Greater men sit on a throne and order tortures; I simply red my hands on their behalf. So I will only observe that Rudolf Elphberg, the untouchable heir, had deserved a prison cell as much as any man in Ruritania, and if he was unjustly imprisoned for these months, perhaps that served a little to balance the years in which he was unjustly free.

I played patience and waited. Night came. The windows of the chateau were open while its inhabitants were awake, and with all the doors open in the Tower for air, I could hear faint laughter. Rupert of Hentzau was making merry, it seemed, as cheerfully and carelessly as though he expected nothing more from the night than a good sleep.

Time passed. The clock struck twelve, and Bersonin drifted into a light doze. It struck one, and I went to the main gate of the Tower to get some air and keep my legs stretched for action. I could see Antoinette's open window, in the chateau over the moat; I saw her standing in the window, silhouetted against the lamplight, and I saw a man's form that was not Michael's come up to her and whisper close.

Hentzau was in her room. I wondered what he was up to.

Faint voices drifted over the moat: Hentzau cajoling, I thought, Antoinette rebuking, and then Michael's harsh, angry voice, loud enough to make out. "What are you doing here, sir?"

A brief argument followed, of which I could not make out the words. It seemed that Michael sent Hentzau packing though, because a few moments later he was standing at the far end of the drawbridge, calling de Gautet loudly. I stepped back into the hall so I should not appear to await him.

"De Gautet, de Gautet, man!" Hentzau shouted, cheerily inconsiderate of any sleepers. "The drawbridge is to be raised. Unless you want a bath before your bed, come along!"

I slipped back down to the lower room, and jumped when I heard gunshots a second later, but the raised, laughing voices told me that it was Hentzau and de Gautet playing the fool shooting at something in the water. If we had not been acting a part I would have had harsh words for them both, since they sounded somewhat tipsy. I hoped Hentzau was, once again, in better control of himself than he seemed.

They sauntered over; the bridge was drawn back, isolating the Tower. De Gautet clattered up the stone stairs to bed, Hentzau assuring him he'd lock the door. I slipped softly out of the room where Bersonin snored and went lightly up to the main door.

Hentzau was there, his coat stripped off, a dim figure in the light of a single candle. He looked round sharply when he saw me, then raised a finger for my attention. I lifted a brow in question. He pointed at himself, then the door, then mimed putting his hands together, paddled his arms, and then moved them up and down.

What? I mouthed.

He rolled his eyes and beckoned me over. I came close, inhaling his smell: wine, candlewax, the faint scent of him.

"Flavia wrote," he breathed in my ear. "The child is found, and safe."

I clenched my fist; I should have liked to shout aloud. Antoinette would have her Lisl back, Michael could now be killed without a moment's concern, and I was ready to take on every overbred bastard in Ruritania and win. I gave Hentzau a fierce grin in lieu of saying all that, and saw his eyes sparkle with the same immense satisfaction in victory, before he pulled my head close again.

"I'm going over. Swim and climb. I left a rope and she's expecting me. I'll wait for Michael and take him."

"No," I said, equally soft. "I'll go."

He shook his head. "You're de Gautet's master; I'm only his match. You need to be on this side to make sure Rassendyll lives. You must, for Flavia. I can take Michael."

"What about all Rassendyll's men?"

"I'm planning to avoid them."

I gave him a look. He shook his head, lips obstinately pressed.

I would be on this side of the moat, facing de Gautet and Bersonin, plus presumably Rassendyll and perhaps others of his party. Hentzau would be on the far side, fighting for Toni and Flavia against Michael's men and the player-king's forces, however many that might prove to be. Each of us would be everyone's enemy. Together we might have stood a chance; fighting separately we were probably so buggered it made the eyes water.

But I had no doubt of what Michael would do when he realised Toni had betrayed him, and every day I had lived past my appointment with Madame la Guillotine was thanks to her. Hentzau had no such obligation and no reason at all to increase his own risk tenfold on her behalf; I found myself stunned and shaken with gratitude that he would do so for her—or even, perhaps, for me.

There was much I could have said, with time and space. As it was, I confined myself to, "Thank you."

He smiled, wry and amused and wonderful. "Be ready. Good luck."

He left his revolver with me, since the water would do it no good. I unlocked the main door and let him out as quietly as possible, then locked it once more behind him. I fancied I heard a faint chuckle and a soft splash.

I retreated to my proper place in the outer room of the dungeon, and wondered what Rassendyll was up to at this moment.

Silence reigned for perhaps fifteen minutes. The clock chimed half past one. *Half an hour to go*, I remember thinking, and at that very second, all hell broke loose.

"Michael! Michael! *Help me!*"

It was Antoinette, audible all the way from the chateau even in my low dungeon room, screaming her lungs out in good earnest, half an hour too fucking early. *What the hell, Toni?* I thought, and a second thought followed on its heels, a bitter one: surely Hentzau could not have truly intended the villainy he was to be accused of, surely he could not have betrayed us both . . .

"Help, Michael! Hentzau!" Toni shrieked, and then, "*Murder!*"

Bersonin sat up, blinking. I couldn't hear anything from over the moat except Toni's screams, certainly not a yell of men, or any sound of attack. Above us, de Gautet gave an exclamation, there was a clatter of footsteps on stone as he ran downstairs and into the hall. "Treachery!" he shouted. "Hentzau attacks the duke!"

The key rattled in the great lock, and a sudden increase in the volume of shouts and screams from the chateau told me de Gautet had flung open the door. "Ho, the bri—" His words were cut off with a scream, a gargle, and a heavy thud.

One down.

Bersonin flung me a wide-eyed look. "Hold the door!" he barked. "I'll—" He darted through to the king's chamber.

The outer door was locked, which did no good since we all carried keys. De Gautet's killer must have found his, for he came down the stairs and I heard the scrape as the key turned.

I took a pace back, blade in hand. The door was thrown open and Rassendyll burst in, bloodied sword in hand. His clothing was soaked, his red hair plastered to his head, and he was shaking—doubtless from cold. It was a warm summer night, but he must have swum the moat and waited for however long outside, seizing his chance when de Gautet opened the door.

We both dropped into fighting stance. "Detchard," he said, eyes locked on mine. "Surrender now. Drop your sword and you may live."

A likely story. "I fear not," I said, and engaged his blade with mine. He disengaged deftly enough. I feinted to the other side, watching his footwork; he realised a little too late, stumbling to catch up. We exchanged attacks and ripostes, testing one another in silence but for the scrape of feet, the clash of steel, the faint screaming from the chateau.

He was a decent swordsman, no more, but he had one great advantage: I didn't want to hurt him, whereas he very much wanted to kill me. He fought with the savagery one might expect, given he was fighting for not just his life, but a crown, and with the desperation of a man who knew that one misstep would be his last.

I upped the tempo of my own movements, pressing him harder but not too hard, needing to conceal that I wasn't trying to finish him. Rassendyll moved back, towards the door that led to the stairs, as though he had it in mind to run; I moved clockwise, forcing him round and away from his chance of escape, wondering what the devil I could do.

I needed to lose this fight without him realising I had chosen to do so, and without giving him a chance to end me. He wore a dagger in his belt and had already cut the throat of a sleeping man, so I did not dare simulate an error and surrender. And whatever I did needed to be done quickly, because he was tiring visibly in his wet clothes and already gasping for breath. He'd had too many State dinners, I concluded.

There was a burst of noise from outside: screaming, excited shouts, and a familiar grinding, screeching sound. Rassendyll evidently recognised it as I did: the drawbridge was being lowered. Soon the Tower would be open to anyone who chose, yet there was still no sound of his men outside. He gave a furious bellow and attacked, a wild slashing frenzy that left him wide open. I set my teeth and let myself be driven back towards the staircase.

"Hold!" Bersonin cried from the king's cell. I had forgotten he was there, and I jumped almost as much as Rassendyll, who swung round, trying to get his back to a wall, his eyes still locked on me. "Hold, I say! I have given the king a drink, Rassendyll." Bersonin's voice was laden with sinister significance. "Only I know the antidote. It will start working in ten minutes. Drop your sword now, or Rudolf dies."

Rassendyll's eyes widened at the threat, but he did not drop his sword, and as the seconds ticked by it became very clear that he was not going to. The player-king had made his decision to play the villain, no excuses or pretences left, and he saw that I saw it. His face reddened visibly, and he let out a cry of rage, and lunged at me with a furious oath.

If he couldn't take Bersonin in that mood, I mistook my man. I attacked without reserve, sending Rassendyll staggering back and stumbling under my onslaught, and used the distance I'd gained to leap away. "Damn your king; I am for Michael. Deal with him, Bersonin!" I shouted, and I fled, slamming the door behind me, turning the key, and leaving it in the lock for good measure.

That was how I left them, the true king, the false, and the poisoner who could be blamed for any villainy, and what Rassendyll did then is a matter for the reader to decide.

The drawbridge had thumped into its resting place as we fought. The door of the Tower was held open by de Gautet's fallen body, and I could see out.

Over the moat, a group of Michael's servants stood in a gaggle by the chateau door. Two or three carried lanterns, illuminating the scene; three or four held pikes, but not in a martial way. They were huddled together behind their weapons, faces agitated, and they gazed at the man who stood in the middle of the drawbridge, sword in hand.

Rupert Hentzau was in his trousers and shirt, both wet; the linen was stained with blood, but his easy, buoyant pose told me that he was either not touched at all or merely scratched. There he stood, holding the bridge with sword in one hand and revolver in the other, and he laughed as he spoke. "Come, now. Any takers? Or will you send Michael out so I can finish the job? Michael, you dog! Michael! If you can stand, come on!" He was blood-drunk, I thought, dizzy with the wild joy of battle. "Michael, you bastard! Come on!"

In answer, Antoinette's voice came, a wild scream. "He's dead! My God, he's dead!"

"Dead!" shouted Hentzau triumphantly. "I struck better than I knew! Down with your weapons there! I'm your master now! Who will gainsay me?"

"Detchard!" Antoinette shrieked. "Detchard, Hentzau has killed your master! *Kill him!*"

Hentzau swung round to see me, and we faced one another on the bridge in the moonlight as we had once faced each other under the sun.

I attacked hard, coming up fast and careless, as though driven by anger. Hentzau parried and riposted in turn, shouting with joy. He had learned well from my teaching, because this was the best match he had ever given me, and this time we fought with sharp and naked swords. Nobody interrupted us; nobody fired a gun. The watchers stood rapt as we fought in savage silence for those few, brief perfect moments, bathed in shadow and moonlight on the bridge: hero, villain, henchman, lover.

Hentzau gave a slight jerk of his head, telling me, *Come closer*. I pressed forwards, and then struck, using the flaconade manoeuvre he had tried on me in our first engagement, so long ago. I made my movements obvious enough that he saw the attack coming, and a wild grin dawned on his face. He parried to the outside, stepping in as he did so, and grabbed my wrist, every bit as brutal and graceless as I had once been with him. The blades grated against one another, and we stood locked together, motionless in a battle of strength, faces close enough to kiss.

"Michael's dead," Hentzau murmured.

"And de Gautet. The player-king is alive."

We pulled apart, spun, attacked again. It felt as though I could read his mind, as though one intelligence choreographed us both in perfect harmony. This was better than fucking, I thought, and would have liked to shout that aloud and watch him laugh.

He met my eyes, a clear message in his own, and we stepped into another close stance, swords locked almost at the hilts. "Under your left arm, over the side," Hentzau said, voice low, eyes full of light. "Play dead. I've a plan. Trust me!"

I leapt away with a cry. Hentzau gave a crow of triumph and attacked furiously.

Our swords clashed, both of us fighting with a wild, reckless glee, awash with all the vigour of victory even as our lives hung in the balance. I wanted to say the hell with it all, to stand side by side on the bridge with my Rupert, my glorious villain, and take on any man who dared oppose us, and it took all my will to keep control. I needed to be seen to die: Rassendyll could not let me live, not having seen him in that moment of self-betrayal. I hoped Hentzau's plan was a good one.

There was a faint sound of shouting and hammering from the other side of the chateau. It must be Rassendyll's men, I realised, arriving at last. Time to go. I met Hentzau's eyes and gave him an opening—not much, but he didn't need much—and his sword shot through my lax guard, sliding under my arm, tearing my coat. Antoinette shrieked from the bank. I froze, let my sword drop from my fingers, took in a long, deep breath to fill my lungs, and toppled sideways over the edge of the drawbridge.

The water was exceedingly cold, and I was hard put not to struggle and splash. I swam deeper instead, expelling a little of my precious air. Nobody would be looking at me with Hentzau making a show of himself on the bridge, the moat was dark under the night-shadow of the Tower, and if I could swim some reasonable distance without breaking the surface, I should be able to escape unobserved. I kicked myself onwards, and something heavy and warm hit my back with an oddly soft impact, knocking me downwards. I flailed in shock, thinking absurdly of dolphins or sharks, and as I struggled I felt an arm across my chest. Legs tangled with mine, and I realised there was a man pulling me down into the depths.

I kicked frantically to turn myself, forcing my eyes open in the sting of the water, and saw a dim white face in the green-black light. It was Rudolf V of Ruritania, a weight attached to his legs, his pallid body sinking into the moat.

I will admit I kicked him off with some urgency. He stared open-eyed at me, arms reaching, and I do not know to this day if he was alive or dead, if it was merely the turbulence of the water moving his limbs, or if Rassendyll had weighted him and put him down the pipe to sink without the courtesy of a coup de grâce. My mind was filled with a half-remembered ghost story of a murderer bearing the corpse of his victim on his back and the dead man slowly strangling him, and the seconds stretched like hours as I pushed the drowned king away from me.

My lungs were burning now, and I swam like hell around the corner of the Tower, swam until my chest felt as though it were caving in and I had to come up for air. I made myself do it slowly and silently, which gave me plenty of time to imagine a man with a gun tracking me as I rose, but I kept my silence, and tried to control my heaving breath as my head broke water.

I could hear the sounds of shouts and arguments now. Antoinette shrieked, voice high and shrill; Hentzau replied, laughing, and then two gunshots rang out in quick succession. Hentzau gave a cry of pain, and something heavy hit the water with a splash.

I made myself swim silently on as the noise from the bank rose. There were shouts and the banging of doors, and now faint gunshots. The king's men approached at last, and we in this damned moat were sitting—or swimming, or drowning—ducks.

I reached the wall of the moat where my black cord dangled and heaved myself out, dripping and shaking. I knew I had to run. I would waste everything Hentzau had done if I turned back to help him now and thus showed I was alive. If he had been fatally, or even badly shot, there was damn all I could do about it. Rassendyll's forces had arrived with firearms, and I had only a couple of knives. And, most of all, I am a mercenary, a henchman, cannon fodder for those whose battles make up the pages of history. Men like me skulk away into the darkness, or die in it. Heroic rescues are for heroes.

And with all that, I did not flee into the woods. I shook the water from my hair and started to run back around the edge of the moat, my inadequate knives in my hands, entirely out of ideas but knowing there was, in the end, nothing else I could do.

I'd taken perhaps three strides when I heard the splashing. Hentzau came around the corner of the Tower, swimming in a thrashing, sideways doggy paddle with nothing like his usual grace, face set and looking very pale against the dark water. He looked up at me with wide-eyed fear that turned to relief as he recognised me, and

I ran back, unlashed my cord, and brought it up to the moat's edge as close to him as I could.

He reached the side a moment later and grasped the rope one-handed. His left arm hung uselessly; his feet scrabbled against the slimy bricks, but he could not lift himself as he needed with just one arm. I knelt on the side, reaching down, set my teeth, put my back into it, and hauled him up that steep side of the moat, pull by painful pull.

He collapsed onto the earth once he managed to get onto the bank, but we had no time to lose. I could hear what sounded like dozens of men on the far side of the Tower, shouting at Michael's servants to put down their pikes, and Rassendyll's voice over them, bellowing orders. They'd start looking for bodies soon.

So I grabbed Hentzau's good arm, and we ran like hell. We ran through the shadows and into the forest, ignoring his wound and our heavy dripping clothes, soaked, silent, and cold, without guns, swords, or supplies, hearing the shouts from Zenda castle for far too long and straining our ears for pursuit. We ran, and when Hentzau could no longer run we walked, I supporting his weight as he stumbled on, he holding my balled-up shirt to his shoulder to staunch the bleeding.

It was a damned long ten miles to the border.

CHAPTER EIGHTEEN

The trick to running for one's life is thinking ahead before it becomes necessary. We had not had much opportunity to do that, otherwise I would have had two horses with saddlebags conveniently waiting in the forest. I had, however, made very sure over the months that I sent most of my generous wages across the border, to my bank and to other locations, and had also left a small bag of necessities at a certain inn (three in fact; I like to hedge my bets). Thus I looked reasonably respectable and had money in my pocket as I hunted up a doctor to remove the bullet from Hentzau's shoulder. The quack advised bed rest; I agreed solemnly, hired two horses, and dragged Hentzau another thirty miles before we next stopped.

It was not a pleasant period all told, particularly not for him, but these things must be endured, and eventually they pass. Three days after the events at the castle, we were comfortably accommodated at a country inn a substantial distance from the Ruritanian border. Hentzau's shoulder had been examined and bound up once more, we had had the extremely large hot meal and two bottles of wine to which we had both been looking forward, and we were at last able to talk of anything except wounds and escape.

Hentzau reclined on the bed to rest his shoulder; I sat at the table, turning my glass in my fingers, watching the evening sun catch the ruby liquid and send spangles of colour over the table, like splashes of blood.

"So," I said. "What the hell happened?"

"Well you may ask," Hentzau said. "All right. You know that I spoke to Antoinette earlier that night. I came to tell her I intended to swim over and wait in her room for two o'clock. And she told me that she had had a message from Flavia, telling her the child was found, and advising her of Rassendyll's full plan."

"Oh, there was a plan, was there? I had started to wonder."

"There was. He'd arranged that Johann would open the front door of the chateau to his forces at two o'clock, just as Antoinette was to start screaming rape. His forces were to take the chateau and kill Michael in the chaos; meanwhile, he was to swim over to the Tower to 'save' the king. All very well for him, but it meant that if I was in the chateau to protect Antoinette from Michael, I would find myself significantly outnumbered. I can't say I was feeling precisely optimistic when I left you to go to her that night."

"And yet you did it," I said. "Rupert, I had wanted to say to you—"

"Nonsense, no need. And be quiet when I'm telling a story. It was, what, around quarter past one when I left you in the Tower? So I came out of the door to swim the moat, and I saw out of the corner of my eye a shape. A man, lurking in the shadows. And I realised it was Rassendyll. He was already there, with the attack not due to start until two."

"*Ah.* Was he indeed."

"I pretended not to see him and swam over—rather wondering if he'd take the chance to put a bullet in my head, I will admit—and climbed up to Antoinette's window. I told her Rassendyll was already there, and we realised this was our chance. We could start the party early."

"Before Rassendyll's forces were ready to attack," I said. "Very nice."

"Thank you," he said demurely. "I thought I might be able to deal with Michael promptly and without interference, get you out of the Tower, and make a clean getaway, all before Rassendyll's forces arrived. So Antoinette started screaming, and Michael duly came bursting in to find me, and we fought." He grimaced. "He wasn't my match, you know. It was unequal. We exchanged a few strokes, he shouting for his men, and I suppose he realised that he didn't stand a chance, because he turned and fled for the door. Only, you see, Antoinette had already got behind him and locked it. Locked him in with me."

"Good for her."

"And then the damnedest thing happened," Hentzau said. "He turned, and the expression on his face—oh, hurt, and bewilderment, and betrayal. He looked devastated, it's the only word. And he reached out a hand towards her and said, 'Antoinette. *Why?*'"

"He— Right," I said. "Of course he did. What did she say?"

"'For Christ's sake, Hentzau, kill him.' So I did."

I nodded. "And then?"

"We decided she would play the grieving widow. I ran downstairs and ordered the drawbridge lowered—it was chaos by then, Antoinette screaming, servants milling, and I was damned glad they didn't have firearms. I held the bridge, and you emerged. What did you do with Rassendyll, by the way?"

"Locked him in with Bersonin and Rudolf."

"Oh, very good. And then you toppled over the side, you see, and that was where it went wrong. We'd agreed that Antoinette would shoot at me, for verisimilitude, and I would shout something caddish yet noble—'I can't kill where I've kissed' was what I had in mind, which I thought rather neat—and flee, leaving her to create chaos, wave the gun around, scream about helping the king, and so on. And it all went to plan, right up to the point the bloody woman fired, and hit me."

"I'm not surprised," I said. "I don't think she's ever used a gun in her life before. Did you even ask her if she could shoot? You posturing idiot."

"Yes, well. And that was that, although I must say I was glad you were there to get me out of that sodding moat, because I could not have done that alone. That was really not a pleasurable swim one-armed."

"Nor was mine," I said, and told him about the king sinking to his watery end.

Hentzau whistled. "Rassendyll killed him, you think? Well, of course he did; King Rudolf the Fifth is alive and well in Strelsau."

We knew that from the newspapers. Ruritanian affairs rarely dominate the front pages anywhere except Ruritania, and sometimes not even there, but the unexplained death of the king's own brother had attracted a certain amount of attention. I was mainly concerned to discover if a hue and cry had been put out for the Duke of Strelsau's killer; so far it seemed not.

"So," Hentzau said. "Now what?"

"For whom? Antoinette should, I hope, have her daughter back. Flavia can manage her own affairs. You and I will need to get further away from Ruritania, I think, for safety's sake. And then, well, the world is your oyster. You're free."

"Some might say I've disgraced my name, abandoned my family, and exiled myself from my native land."

"That's what I mean," I said. "You're young, healthy, a damned good swordsman, and have nothing left to lose. It's quite a position to start from, take my word for it. And you did want adventure."

"Indeed I did, and now I shall have all that I want. As a seasoned adventurer, Jasper, would you care to show me the ropes for a little while? With no obligation, needless to say."

"None at all," I agreed. "Go off on your own as and when you choose, just as I will. But until then . . . well, why not? There are plenty of two-man jobs out there, and we do work well together."

"We do," he agreed. "And I can think of a few two-man jobs that I want done in here, if it comes to that."

"With your shoulder?"

"Be damned to my shoulder," he said. "Work around it, that's what you're good at. Come here."

And that is my tale done. Or almost so, since I am reminded readers may wish to know what happened next.

Antoinette was reunited with Lisl just two days after Michael's death. Flavia kept her word as to her protection and even appointed a steward to help Toni untangle her affairs and retrieve the funds Michael had kept from her, as well as his many gifts of jewellery and the extensive wardrobe. Since she had also taken advantage of the chaos to help herself to anything valuable and portable, Toni emerged from her affair with Michael a sadder, wiser, but mostly very much richer woman. She gave it out that she was retiring from the world in mourning for her lost duke, and settled down with her daughter in a small town in southern France, only visiting the larger cities occasionally to keep her hand in.

Lisl Mauban has grown into a remarkable and sharply intelligent young woman. She had an excellent education, in addition to which I taught her to fuzz cards and use a knife, and Hentzau taught her to shoot, not without some sarcastic remarks to her mother on the subject. Toni taught her not to trust a man as far as she could throw him, and then undermined her lesson to everyone's surprise, including her own, by marrying the local doctor. He appears to be a thoroughly decent, gentle man who worships her, and she is quietly and entirely happy with him. Hentzau and I attended her wedding, attempting to look respectable with questionable success.

Rudolf Rassendyll emerged from the Tower that long-ago night with Bersonin dead and no trace of the prisoner he had supposedly come to rescue. I dare say he told a good story to Colonel Sapt; I dare say Sapt wanted to believe it. I don't know what went on behind closed doors thereafter, but Rassendyll-as-Rudolf married Princess Flavia in a grand ceremony in Strelsau, and immediately appointed her Queen in her own right, sharing the business of government with him in equal authority.

There was, of course, the problem of getting rid of Rudolf Rassendyll the Englishman, now that he had to become Rudolf V of Ruritania permanently. Rassendyll solved this by returning to England to show himself in his true identity for a few weeks every year, presenting himself as increasingly reclusive each time, and finally "retiring from the world" for good.

Perhaps six years into his reign, it was reported that the king was suffering from some persistent ailment, as his previous debauched lifestyle finally caught up with him. His condition did not cause a constitutional crisis, since by then it had become apparent to all that Flavia was the ruler, with Rudolf as mere consort and figurehead. The king confined himself, or was confined, to ceremonial appearances only; soon enough he started turning up to public events drunk and resentfully muttering; and a short time thereafter he expired of what was said to be an apoplexy in his sleep. I do wonder if Rassendyll found his crown worth the price he paid for it.

He had given Flavia two healthy daughters by then, and there is no question but that Ruritania's next monarch will be a queen, especially since Flavia is generally agreed to be the wisest and most forward-looking ruler Ruritania has had in many generations, as well as being an exceedingly bad woman to cross.

In his spare time, of which he had plenty, Rassendyll wrote a highly unreliable account of his adventures which was widely circulated after his death. He supposedly wrote it as a plausible explanation of what had happened to him that summer, changing only the ending to preserve the royal family's secret and give his own family a tale to believe. But in truth I think he wrote it for himself, to tell the tale as he wished it had been. In that version (which, as I have said, is riddled with inaccuracies, impossibilities, and unlikelihoods far beyond the truth), Rassendyll is a self-sacrificing hero who gives up love and throne for the sake of the true and legitimate king whose life he saved, and Flavia is a simpering, passive cipher who adores him. Rudolf V survives to reclaim his throne and his bride; I, a minor henchman, die ignominiously, slipping on the blood of my innocent victim; and Rupert of Hentzau stands alone on the pages as a glorious, reckless embodiment of adventure. Let me quote Rassendyll's (entirely fictional) description of his last sight of Rupert Hentzau, and ask yourself what Rudolf Rassendyll—false king, cousin-killer, outmanoeuvred and trapped like a shop dummy on a meaningless throne—wished his life to have been.

Leaning forward, he tossed his hair off his forehead and smiled, and said: "Au revoir, Rudolf Rassendyll!"

Then, with his cheek streaming blood, but his lips laughing and his body swaying with ease and grace, he bowed to me . . . and rode away at a gallop.

And I watched him go down the long avenue, riding as though he rode for his pleasure and singing as he went, for all there was that gash in his cheek.

Once again he turned to wave his hand, and then the gloom of thickets swallowed him and he was lost from our sight. Thus he vanished—

reckless and wary, graceful and graceless, handsome, debonair, vile, and unconquered. And I flung my sword passionately on the ground . . .

I could almost find it in my heart to pity Rassendyll, you know.

It only remains to tell what Hentzau and I did next. Well, we adventured. We roamed Europe for a year and more, fucking and fighting as we pleased; we parted when our wanderlust took us in different directions, and met again in new cities. I did not see him for three years once, when he fell hopelessly in love with a prima donna in the Imperial Opera of Warsaw. They were a well-matched pair in every way; she led him a merry dance until he finally lost her affections to the King of Bohemia. Nobody at all heard of him for a few months after that, and then he reappeared as though he had never been away, but with a few new lines around his eyes, and told me a South African hunter of his acquaintance was putting together a party for a somewhat unusual expedition and would I like to accompany him.

So we have rolled on through the years, happy in each other's company, not troubled at parting because we will doubtless meet again. It has been well over two decades now, and I am unquestionably becoming too old and grizzled for this life. And yet, like an idiot, I write this on the Orient Express bound for Constantinople, and for trouble.

Once again, this is all Hentzau's fault. He introduced me to a young man last year, the son of some Scottish lord, all air and fire and nerves, and the pair of us spent a highly satisfactory week in a hotel room giving him an education. In between bouts, we exchanged enough conversation to become rather fond of the youth, one Sandy Arbuthnot, before he headed off to seek further adventures. Evidently he found them, since he is currently held prisoner in some Cappadocian fortress. He managed to smuggle a letter out, which eventually reached Hentzau, and so we go east to a land neither of us knows, to rescue a pretty Scot with a death wish.

It is, I may add, my sixtieth birthday today. Hentzau, still reading over my shoulder as he has been from the start, says he has no intention of allowing me to age any further; I cannot imagine I will have the opportunity if we carry on like this (and yes, Rupert, I know I always say that).

Ah well. This is a ridiculous way for an ageing swordsman to go on, but one must help one's companions in life, or what else is there? And it should, at least, be interesting.

Jasper Detchard
Constantinople or thereabouts
19—

AUTHOR'S NOTE

I feel I ought to apologise to Anthony Hope, author of *The Prisoner of Zenda*. It's one of my favourite (problematic favourite) Victorian pulp novels. I hugely enjoyed inverting his story and borrowing Rupert of Hentzau, one of the great charm-villains of all time, and I feel slightly bad for being so rude about his hero.

That said, during the course of writing this book, I realised that Hope had given the ancient keep of Zenda a drawbridge that opened from both sides, causing me endless trouble, so let's just say we're even.

Huge thanks to Chas Lovett, who spent ages delving into Munich geography to help me get one line right, and to Alexis Hall, who sorted out my swordfights like a maestro.

ALSO BY KJ CHARLES

Wanted, A Gentleman

A Charm of Magpies world
The Magpie Lord
A Case of Possession
Flight of Magpies
Jackdaw
A Queer Trade
Rag and Bone

Society of Gentlemen
The Ruin of Gabriel Ashleigh
A Fashionable Indulgence
A Seditious Affair
A Gentleman's Position

Non-Stop Till Tokyo
Think of England
The Secret Casebook of Simon Feximal

Sins of the Cities
An Unseen Attraction
An Unnatural Vice
An Unsuitable Heir

Green Men
Spectred Isle

ABOUT THE AUTHOR

KJ Charles is a writer and freelance editor. She lives in London with her husband, two kids, an out-of-control garden, and an increasingly murderous cat.

KJ writes mostly romance, mostly queer, frequently historical, and usually with some fantasy or horror in there.

Find her on Twitter @kj_charles, pick up free reads on her website at kjcharleswriter.com, get the infrequent newsletter at kjcharleswriter.com/newsletter, or join her Facebook group, KJ Charles Chat, for sneak peeks and exclusives.

She is represented by Courtney Miller-Callihan at Handspun Literary.

Printed in Great Britain
by Amazon